Moondust Lake

Books by Davis Bunn

Miramar Bay

Firefly Cove

Moondust Lake

Moondust Lake

DAVIS BUNN

KENSINGTON BOOKS
www.kensingtonbooks.com

KENSINGTON BOOKS are published by

Kensington Publishing Corp.
119 West 40th Street
New York, NY 10018

All Kensington titles, imprints, and distributed lines are available at special quantity discounts for bulk purchases for sales promotion, premiums, fund-raising, educational, or institutional use. Special book excerpts or customized printings can also be created to fit specific needs. For details, write or phone the office of the Kensington Special Sales Manager: Attn. Special Sales Department. Kensington Publishing Corp, 119 West 40th Street, New York, NY 10018. Phone: 1-800-221-2647.

Library of Congress Card Catalogue Number: 2018952787

ISBN-13: 978-1-4967-0835-9
ISBN-10: 1-4967-0835-0
First Kensington Hardcover Edition: January 2019

ISBN-13: 978-1-4967-0837-3 (e-book)
ISBN-10: 1-4967-0837-7 (e-book)

10 9 8 7 6 5 4 3 2 1

Printed in the United States of America

This book is dedicated to:

Debbie Macomber

For her inspiration, her wisdom, and her friendship most of all

Acknowledgments

A number of people have gone out of their way to assist me in learning the ins and outs of psychotherapy and counseling. One in particular must be named here: Dr. Nicholas Pediaditakis has been a friend and patient guide for years. It was because of his openhearted passion for the field that I studied psychology, both in undergraduate and business school. I never fully engaged with this discipline and had no interest in making it a profession. But the compassion and drive and brilliant insight that defined Nicholas lives in so many people, and they have in many respects defined me as an author.

Thanks also to Jason and Jean Marie Peltier, dear friends who introduced me to the farming world of California's Central Valley. And to my dear wife, Isabella, who has always considered California the home she most loves, regardless of where she has landed.

My sincerest appreciation goes to Wendy McCurdy and all the Kensington team. They are, without reservation, the best.

Chapter 1

Buddy Helms ran through a pewter dawn. The sky was gray and wrapped in clouds like shredded yarn. The sidewalk was old and pitted and unbalanced. It had rained in the night, the drops drumming hard enough to wake him twice. There was no telling how deep the puddles were, so he ran around them in uneven, jerky steps. His breathing was as out of synch as his pace. All the other Sunday-morning joggers stayed on the other side of the street. The newer sidewalk was smooth as the growing light. Buddy was the only one running over here. He liked the solitude and he liked the challenge. That was as good a motto for his life as he could come up with today.

He always ran over here when he was on his own, beneath the ancient California cottonwoods. The road skirted one of San Luis Obispo's earliest neighborhoods, and all the houses on this side were over a century old. On the other side stretched four new town-house developments. The last one was a victim of the recession, the entrance a raw mouth of glistening clay. A new billboard had been planted that week, making the rain-slick announcement that the buildings would rise under new management, that the bad times were over. California's central coast was shrugging off the forest fires and deluges and mudslides. San Luis Obispo was back on track—pushing and growing and claiming the future that everybody wanted to call golden.

Buddy preferred this side of the road because there was so little left of the old town. Besides which, Buddy had to break his stride over there as well. He was different from other folks, even here, when runners puffed early morning greetings. He was not out here to jog. From the instant Buddy emerged from his glistening new town house, Buddy Helms *ran*.

His phone buzzed in the pocket of his felt vest. Buddy did not check the readout because he didn't need to. One of his friends was either up early or making a final call before the postdawn collapse, wanting to know why he hadn't shown up. Again. Buddy had no interest in divulging the truth—at least, not yet and not to them.

After months of struggle and worry, he had finally landed a deal on Friday. *The* deal. The clincher. The one he had been hunting for three long years. Ever since the most recent downturn had brought his father's company to its knees.

Other firms might call theirs a family concern. But the Helms Group was his father's. Make no mistake. And Buddy's new deal meant a return to profit. Finally. After a long, nightmarish struggle that had cost them dearly. Buddy most of all.

That Friday, when the deal had closed and the ink dried, Buddy had dropped the contract by his parents' house, then had driven home in a stupor. He had slept sixteen hours straight, and woken so groggy he could barely make a delayed meal, much less think about joining his pals.

Soon he left the city behind and entered the tougher phase of his seventeen-mile run. Buddy Helms had four circuits laid out with his home as a starting point. This one took him southwest, into the hills separating his hometown from Avila Beach. The trail was dangerous in the dry season, when rattlesnakes hid in shadows, and coyotes came down from the high ground in search of food. There was a different risk now, with every storm bringing the threat of further mudslides. Even so, Buddy loved the empty miles, the throwback to an era when this section of California was known as the Wild Coast.

When he arrived back, Buddy stepped onto his veranda and dropped onto the exercise mat. Two hundred sit-ups, two hundred push-ups, then up and onto the bar for a hundred pull-ups. No jerking. Smooth and clean. He returned to the mat and began a kata, a stylized fighting routine that Buddy used as a final stretch.

Midway through, the sliding doors opened across the central pool from his own home, and his newest neighbor stepped onto her veranda. Her kimono-style robe revealed a long expanse of slender legs bare to the cold spring morning. Buddy had noticed her before. There was a lot about this raven-haired beauty to notice. She cradled her steaming mug and eyed him with the cool gaze of a cat studying a bowl of fresh cream. Buddy stepped inside and shut his glass to a temptation he definitely did not need. Especially not today.

Buddy showered and dressed. Brooks Brothers navy suit, starched pale blue shirt, rep tie. Polished black loafers. Out the door, smile a meaningless hello to the raven-haired beauty as she drove past in her Lexus, into his Jeep, and off.

His sister lived in a ground-floor apartment carved from a mock-Victorian home that they both had loved at first sight. Carey's portion had a front parlor with a castellated tower of pale yellow brick. Nobody knew where the color had come from. The bricks had definitely not been fired from the fingernail-red central-coast clay. Some developer had recently decided the two-acre yard would make the perfect site for a fifteen-thousand-square-foot altar to some nouveau riche ego. But Carey and her neighbors had taken their fight to city hall and won.

Carey emerged from the front door before Buddy cut his

motor. Which meant the day was not a good one. His assumption was confirmed by how Ricardo slipped from the house behind her. His sister's latest flame was from the Dominican Republic, by way of Los Angeles, a blade-thin mestizo and impossibly handsome. When Buddy had first met the man, he had assumed Ricardo was either gay or an assassin. Instead, he was another in his sister's long line of musician lovers. But there was something about this one that rubbed Buddy wrong. Ricardo leaned on the front banister and smoked, his dark gaze smoldering with his cigarette. Buddy had learned the hard way to keep his opinions to himself, even when Carey slipped into the car and said, "Give me a minute."

"No problem."

They drove in silence, the tires humming the high tune of wet asphalt. Buddy stopped by the Starbucks closest to her home and went in for two coffees. A black Americano for him, hers a hodgepodge of caramel and chocolate and the calories she normally refused herself. When he returned, she took a sip, sighed, then leaned over and kissed his cheek.

"Good morning, brother."

"Better?"

"Mmmm." She sipped again, then asked, "Did you land the deal?"

"They signed on Friday."

She gave his shoulder a mock slap. "Why didn't you call me?"

"Didn't have the strength to lift the receiver."

"Does Pop know?"

"I dropped the contract off around midnight. Went home. Slept forever."

"Did he call?"

"Not a peep."

"He's probably . . ." She tried to drown the thought in her cup.

"Still trying to find something to complain about," he finished for her. "But he won't. The deal is solid gold. It doubles the group's income, sis. And returns us to profit."

"Stand back, folks." Her smile was genuine. "The genie is out of the bottle."

He pulled into the church parking lot, waved to a family he'd known all his life, and asked, "Ready?"

Her smile went from open to compressed. "I can't let you face this alone, right?"

"Not today."

"That's him, there on the church's top step." Preston Sturgiss pointed through the front windshield. "Jack Helms."

The City Community Church was a massive edifice that dominated the intersection. The man that Preston pointed to looked pretty much as her cousin had described, stern and unbending. Kimberly asked, "If you dislike him so, why are you having lunch with them?"

"I told you. Beth asked me."

"His wife," Kimberly recalled.

"The driving force behind our new counseling center," Preston confirmed. "In her own quiet, sweet way this lady is a mover and a shaker."

"And Beth Helms asked you to set up an appointment with me. A woman she's never met. Before I've even shown up for my first day."

"Right. That's her standing beside him."

Jack Helms stood on the church's high veranda, showing all newcomers the granite exterior of a man who lived to judge. Beth Helms was a slender woman with a serene expression and a smile for everyone who passed. "What is she like?"

"A saint."

"She'd have to be, if the husband is as bad as you say."

"The one time I met Jack Helms, he declared that he had been against the counseling project from the very outset." Preston leaned forward and squinted at the stern old man, like he was taking aim. "He said their church had no business doing anything with Catholics, much less go into the counseling business."

Preston's family members were Catholics and had been for generations beyond count. Kimberly had always assumed she would live out her days within the very same community. Until her world had been upended, and so many of her assumptions had been stripped away. "You could go into private practice," she pointed out. "It's not too late."

"Yes, it is." Preston gave her the smile that had carried her through so much. The one that said he understood everything she was not saying. "You're going to be fine, Kimberly. This is a great place. And so are the people. Most of them, anyway." He rose from the car and pointed across the intersection. "The Catholic church I attend is on the other side of that park."

Kimberly said, "You don't need to stay with me."

"I want to introduce you around." As they started for the steps, he stopped abruptly and said softly, "Here come two of the Helms children. Buddy and Carey. There's a third, a daughter. But she hasn't been home in forever. Beth goes out to see her once a year."

"Should you be telling me this?"

"I explained all that. Beth would prefer to work with a female counselor. I told her about you. She's requested an appointment."

"Preston, I'm still not certain . . ."

She stopped then. It felt to Kimberly as though she had been arrested. Just gripped by the heart and jerked to silence. The son of Jack Helms passed in front of where they stood. Buddy Helms carried himself like an athlete, a bounce to his stride and a rawboned strength that emanated from him like an animal scent. Kimberly had always liked that sense of unrefined power in a man. Which was a pity, really, since it had led to so much pain.

Buddy Helms was also intensely handsome. A number of the other women noticed as well. Many of the female churchgoers glanced his way. She doubted Buddy ever noticed. There was something about the way he carried himself that left Kimberly fairly certain he was unaware of his looks. She knew from experience that some men discounted their ability to draw female attention. Such rare males had always belonged to other, more fortunate women.

Buddy passed so close she could see a small indentation below his left eye, probably the result of some childhood injury. He had big hands and massive shoulders and short-cropped dark hair. There was a jewel-like quality to his gray gaze, like precious stones had been wrapped in a towel and shattered with furious blows. And there on the top stair stood the man with the hammer. Of that, Kimberly had no doubt.

But that was not why she went silent. Kimberly found herself gripped by a sudden thought, one so powerful it might as well have been scripted across the gray shield of clouds overhead. Had the impression been any less formidable, she would have laughed out loud. The thought was, *You are going to marry this man.*

Preston said something and led her up the stairs. Beth Helms saw their approach and came down to meet them. Preston introduced them, and Kimberly heard herself give some sort of response. But it was all she could do to keep herself from gaping across the veranda at Buddy Helms.

Then a hand touched her arm, drawing her back to where she stood. Beth Helms gave her such a knowing gaze Kimberly felt herself flush. But all that the woman said to her was "Can I come see you Tuesday?"

She heard herself say, "I'm sure that will be fine."

Beth thanked her and rejoined the family. Preston held back a moment longer, then led Kimberly inside.

She did not hear a word of the service. She was too busy arguing with whatever absurd force had insisted upon shattering her Sunday by planting such a ridiculous notion in her brain.

Preston's family had taken Kimberly home the night her own

parents had died in the crash. She had been eleven at the time. Gradually it had sunk in that she had not come there for a night, but for life. Her favorite aunt and uncle and cousin had become the only family she had left. Preston's mother had always considered Kimberly the daughter she was unable to have. Kimberly had been saved from the worst agony of loss by people who had nurtured and sheltered and brought her into womanhood with love.

As a teen Kimberly had fostered vague notions of going into medicine, then happily cast them aside during her final year at university when she fell in love. She and Jason wed the week after they graduated. Their marriage lasted a week less than two years. The morning after she announced that she was pregnant, the love of her young life did not come home from work. Gradually a waking nightmare drew its cruel cloak over her world. First had come the revelation that he had not been faithful. Then four months into the pregnancy Kimberly lost the child. Then she was served with divorce papers. And through the veiled chatter of supposed friends, she learned that her husband was living with Kimberly's college roommate and former best friend. Whom he now claimed he had loved all along.

The divorce final, her home a wasteland, Kimberly had moved back in with Preston's parents, who by this point were her own as well. Preston had urged her to put her sympathetic nature to good use, and Kimberly had returned to school for a degree in counseling. To her surprise, she proved remarkably adept at drawing out much-needed confessions from her patients. She suspected it was because nothing about human nature had the power to surprise her any longer.

With a start Kimberly realized the church service had ended and people were leaving. Preston gave her the knowing look for a second time that morning and asked, "Everything okay?"

"I'm still wondering if I'm doing the right thing. Coming down here and taking this job."

"Will you trust me if I say that you are?"

She liked the concern in his gaze. And the need. For he was almost as lonely as she was. "I'll try."

"Good girl. Shall I drive you back?"

"I'd rather walk."

"There's food in the fridge. And you'll pass a supermarket on your way—"

"I'm a big girl, Preston. I won't starve."

As they proceeded up the central aisle, she found herself only a few people removed from Buddy Helms. Kimberly repressed a shudder. The very idea of becoming involved with anyone repulsed her. The last thing she needed was another reason to run away.

CHAPTER 2

As usual, Buddy's exercise routine blanketed him in an endorphin-induced peace so strong he could ignore his father's cold dismissal. For the past nine years this had been Jack Helms's standard Sunday face. Buddy's father stood on the upper stair and showed the arriving parishioners his Mount Rushmore expression. Stony and unbending. The face of the conservative Evangelical, the guardian of the doors. No hint of wrongness would ever be permitted to enter. Nowadays Jack Helms served as the church's righteous judge. The man who lived to find fault and condemn.

Okay. So it did hurt.

Eight months of work and worry, and the deal was done. Even here at church the old man might at least have welcomed him with a "job well done." Buddy had hoped for the call that had never woken him the day before. He should not have expected anything different now.

Buddy emerged into the pale wash of a March noon, stood beside his mother and shook hands, then trooped back to the car with his sister. He had a lot of experience at ignoring slights. He should have been prepared.

When they pulled up in front of the house, Carey demanded, "What's the matter?"

"Same old."

"You know he wouldn't say anything at church."

"He didn't call yesterday."

"Buddy . . ."

He opened his door. "It's fine."

Only it wasn't, and it didn't get better. For once, the dawn workout failed him. Buddy helped his mother set the table and felt the ache stab him every time his father came into view. Jack Helms sat in the front parlor with the head of the new counseling service that several local churches were jointly sponsoring. Buddy wondered how Preston Sturgiss had gotten hooked into joining them. Jack often dragged somebody home from church. It gave him a fresh audience. Over lunch his sister mouthed the same words that had made Buddy smile ever since Jack had undergone his grim transformation.

Carey was mild and caring like their mother, but somehow a secret trace of mayhem had crept into her genes. She would never confront her father openly. But behind his back, safe from his wrath, she lived a peculiar and secret rebellion. Her latest Caribbean lover was one example. Or the way she silently framed the words around her spoon, or down at her plate, never actually looking at Buddy, knowing he saw her whisper, *the Washington rant, the Democrat rant, the liberal-media rant, the gay rant.*

The last was cut short by the phone. Buddy was out of his chair before the first ring ended. His father snapped, "Let it ring. That's what the answering machine is for."

But he wasn't going to answer the phone. Buddy rose because he needed to draw a decent breath. He walked into the kitchen, and realized his hands were shaking as he lifted the receiver. "Helms residence."

His sister asked, "Has Pop finished with the liberal televised conspiracy to turn our daughters into Democrats?"

Buddy turned his back to the dining room. "Not yet."

"Then he must have an outside cheering section. Who is it today, his banker? The company lawyer?"

"The church is helping to set up a therapy center."

"I bet Pop had some choice bits to say about that. Something that started with 'over my dead body.'"

Buddy's older sister lived in Vancouver. Sylvie had tried Maui first, but her restlessness had turned the island into a semitropical prison. She hated Vancouver's weather, but loved the distance between her and San Lu. Sylvie ran a successful wine-importing business. With her female lover. Another pair of items he and Carey and their mother saw no need to mention to their father.

Buddy asked, "Why are you calling this early?"

"Haven't been to bed yet. We hosted a big do last night." He heard the flick of a lighter, and his sister's already deep voice thickened with smoke. "Put Mom on the phone."

Buddy's mind slipped back to an earlier time. Back before his father had undergone the seismic shift, and theirs had been a happy home. Jack Helms had always possessed some jagged edges. The man loathed being questioned or contradicted, especially by his own family. But so long as everyone had lived by Jack's unspoken rules, he had been a kind and giving man. The odd flashes of blind rage came and went like spring tornados, wreaking havoc and then disappearing into memory. Until the change.

The year Sylvie had turned twenty-one, she went through some seismic shift. Why exactly, Buddy had no idea. Suddenly his older sister decided she was no longer going to live by Jack's rules. Instead, Sylvie thrived on defying her father. She baited the bull day after day until Jack Helms lost his balance entirely. And became the man he was today.

Buddy had grown up wanting nothing more than to work at his father's side. He had spent years convinced he could not only measure up to Jack's high standards, but restore the balance to their relationship and his family. Even now, as he gripped the receiver and listened to the monotonous drone from the dining room, he yearned for those earlier dreams.

His sister interrupted, asking, "Did you hear what I said?"

"Now isn't a good time."

"My sweet diplomat of a brother. When is it a good time in that house?"

"Dad won't like it."

"I never did understand why you try to get along with the beast that man has become." His sister slurred the words, explaining why she gave voice to the hidden. "Fat lot of good it did you . . ."

Buddy cut the connection, then reconnected and hit the 1 button and set down the receiver.

He walked back down the hallway, but did not reenter the dining room. He stood where his father couldn't see him and surveyed the scene. Preston Sturgiss, the young therapist, wore the deer-in-headlights expression Buddy had seen all too often. His mother, the gentlest soul Buddy had ever known, sat beside her husband, smiling the same beatific smile she had used to soothe any number of "Jack-fits." That was Carey's word for it, the endless spewing of courtly ire, as though speaking softly excused him from remaining perpetually filled with bile. Nowadays Jack Helms would not have been satisfied even if he could reorder the world's spin. Carey sat beside her mother, a distant, glazed look to her eyes. She had her mother's beauty, the sculpted features and auburn hair, the same strong carriage and the full lips. Buddy doubted she heard a single word.

He entered the room and announced, "I have to go."

Jack bridled. "I haven't dismissed you yet."

Buddy looked down at his father and knew Jack Helms had brought this specific man home, this specific day, so that he would have an excuse not to speak about the specific issue that Buddy had spent the past six years waiting to hear. That he had done a good job. That he had lived up to expectations. That he was worthy of his father's praise.

His mother said, "Buddy?"

He felt the snap deep inside his soul. He had heard of this from athletes, who described a parting tendon that way, the sound coming up through the body rather than through the ears. All Buddy could say for certain was that any reason to stay had just been eviscerated.

He leaned over and kissed his mother's cheek. "Thanks for lunch. I'll call you tomorrow. Coming, sis?"

His father's ire followed them as together they walked out the massive front door. The oak portal was peaked at the top, like a medieval entryway, with cast-iron handle and twisted bars shaped over a small opening at face level. The door spoke volumes about the man who lived inside, the stalwart determination to defend his world against everything he judged to be impure.

Buddy crossed the porch and stopped by the top stair. He stared about, seeing it with new eyes. The front veranda had six rockers painted to match the railing. The front yard was framed by blooming trees, three crepe myrtles and five Yoshino cherries. He studied the rocker he had claimed as a child, remembering how he had loved sitting there, eagerly awaiting his father's arrival, dreaming of a future when Buddy and Jack would return home from work together.

His sister called from the car, "You coming?"

He patted the railing and descended the stairs. He walked around and opened her door, something he had never done before. His sister's only response was to squint at him. As he slipped behind the wheel, he spotted his mother standing in the window. Buddy was not surprised she had noticed the change. Beth Helms had always been a sensitive and observant woman. It was how she survived.

Buddy started the car, pulled from the curb, then said to his sister, "I'm never going back."

CHAPTER 3

For the first time in over a year, Buddy skipped his Monday-morning workout entirely. Normally, the only thing that kept him from sweating through the dawn was a fever. Today, however, he dressed and drove straight to work.

The Helms Group was housed in a series of brick structures with tall flagpoles fronting the admin center. The complex held a vaguely military air, which was no doubt his father's intention. Some of their younger employees called it the Bunker.

The wind whipped that morning, and the flags snapped nervously, as though fearing the outburst that was soon to come. Buddy went straight to the finance division, where the chief was already at his desk. The head accountant shaped his days by the FILO rule—first in, last out. Buddy had long since stopped trying to beat him in. He rapped on the open door, asked, "Got a minute?"

"Did you get it?" Meaning the deal.

"They signed over dinner on Friday."

"Then I can give you all day." He was a portly guy, late

fifties, not a hard angle to his body or his opinions. Which was one reason why he had survived this long.

Buddy said, "I want to reward my team."

"Sounds reasonable. What does the old man say?"

"I'll tell him after it's done."

"Buddy, no, wait."

"You can either help me or you can give me the checkbook in your top drawer and claim I took it before you got in. But this is happening. Now. Before Pop shows up."

The guy made a face like a man trying to swallow a peach pit. "But *why*?"

"My team sweated fourteen weeks of blood over this. I'm not giving Pop a chance to belittle what they've achieved." Buddy walked around, opened the drawer, pulled out the wide leather-bound check holder. "Got a pen?"

The man handed it over. "How much are you . . ."

"Ten thousand for the team members. Five for the assistants."

"That's . . ."

"A hundred thousand even."

"Jack will go through the roof."

"Probably." Buddy signed his father's name, something he had been doing for years, and tore off the first check. "Do something useful. Make out the envelopes."

Buddy found an exquisite sadness in the process of going around his team's section, leaving the envelopes at the center of each empty desk. Serena, his secretary, arrived just as he finished his rounds. Jack had tried to foist his own choice for secretary on Buddy, a dowdy beast with a penchant for sniffing at his every request. Buddy had eased her down into the accounts-receivable department, where she struck fear and trembling into every deadbeat payee. Buddy's secretary was a matronly Latina with a saint's voice, calm and warm and steadying. Serena mothered his team and showed a woman's wisdom in every crisis. Buddy especially like handing her the envelope, watching her open it, seeing the shock.

"Five thousand dollars? Really?"

"I wish it was more."

"I can't thank you enough."

"You took the words out of my mouth." He started for his office. "No interruptions."

Rolodexes had gone the way of Day-Timers. But the next two hours were spent winging through the professional contacts in his computer. Buddy worked the phone preparing for what came next. While there was still time.

He was still not ready when his father stormed in. Buddy felt his insides congeal with the familiar icy dread.

His father was dressed in Monday grays—slate-dark suit, woven black tie, heavy lace-up shoes with toes like curved mirrors. Jack's eyes were the color of an Arctic winter, gray and bone-hard. The only tint was the high pink to his cheekbones, a sure sign of fury. "What have you gone and done?"

Buddy set down the phone. He didn't bother with silent reminders to toughen up. Stand tall. Stay cool. He would not disgrace the day with fables. Buddy replied, "What you should have done yourself."

His father gave him the wide-eyed expression of the wronged man, the citizen innocent of all fault, the one who had been granted every reason to show a righteous rage. "You passed around a hundred thousand dollars of *my money*?"

Buddy could hear the same tremors in his voice that had infected every such confrontation since he had started work here. "It should be twice that."

Jack Helms stalked the carpet in front of his desk. Getting ready to explode. Turning the space into his very own stage. The longer he fumed, the more powerful the outburst that followed.

Through his rising tension, Buddy felt pierced by the same clarity as he had experienced the day before. He realized that since Jack had gone through the drastic shift of nine years back, his father had increasingly come to like such moments. It was his way of manipulating people to do what he wanted. Buddy felt vaguely ashamed of himself for having spent years living in a past that no longer existed.

For the first time as his father's employee, Buddy did not wait for the storm. He said, "You knew I was going to do this."

That stopped Jack in midstride. Or perhaps it was Buddy's tone. Jack had most likely heard the change himself. There was none of the usual apology, one tiny fraction removed from begging.

Jack hissed, *"What did you say?"*

"My team saved the company. They needed to be rewarded. But you'd never do it yourself. So now you can yell at me and pretend—"

"Are you *insane*? Have you gone *completely* out of your skinny little head?"

Buddy did another new thing. Not even planning it. Just knowing he had to. For himself. For the time to come. He rose to his feet. Walked around his desk. Entered into his father's space. "No. I'm not."

Such an act of defiance was utterly incomprehensible. Jack Helms stabbed the air between them. "You will *sit down.*"

Buddy remained where he was. "If you don't like it, fire me."

"If I don't . . ." Jack halted because of the knock on the door and the appearance of Buddy's secretary. "Get *out.*"

"Sorry, sir, it's the president of Morgan Mutual. He says it's urgent."

Jack Helms blinked slowly. Doing a lizard thing. Swallowing the rage down deep. Turning back into the man in rigid control. He had no choice. A Monday-morning call from the company's chief banker could not be put off. He did not look directly at Buddy, as though to look directly at his son risked his losing it totally. "My office. Five minutes."

Serena waited until the company president had stormed away to ask, "Do I have to give back the money?"

"No. Of course not." Buddy returned to his desk and forced his trembling hand to clench the phone. "But, Serena . . ."

"Yes?"

"Tell everyone to deposit their checks immediately."

Buddy rushed through his final three calls. Then he printed off his newly revised CV, a document that had gathered electronic dust for far too long. As he entered the central bull pen, he told his secretary, "I'm gone for the rest of the day."

"What about the Monday staff meeting?"

"I won't make it." He started off, then backtracked to her desk. Buddy pulled a sheet of paper from her printer and the pen from his jacket pocket. He wrote out the three words in huge letters. *Praise your team.*

Buddy folded it lengthwise and gave it to her, saying, "Give this to Pop. Tell him I left so the task will be easier for him."

CHAPTER 4

Buddy's first two meetings were with headhunters he knew from the gym. They had chided him for years to leave, and now found themselves challenged to do what they had long offered. He used their discussions as testing grounds, which was important. Vital.

Buddy Helms had never before applied for a job.

When he arrived at the third meeting, he was as ready as he would ever be.

Buddy had known Bernard Featherstone his entire life. He was a jovial member of the community church's leadership, a man whose smile carried a remarkable steely glint. His smooth voice was capable of pouring an unguent over the most heated of discussions. Even Jack Helms had been brought under control. Occasionally.

But that was not why Buddy had saved him for last.

Bernard Featherstone had trained as a lawyer. He had practiced as a corporate litigator for a dozen years, until his combative edge had almost cost him his wife and his family. He had left the law and entered headhunting, finding jobs for other lawyers. Eight years earlier, he had been hired by the nation's largest executive-search firm and charged to set up an office in Santa Barbara. Nowadays Bernard only worked with the top-drawer clients, senior executives who needed serious stroking, and whose salary and packages had made Bernard very rich. Buddy was the only man in Bernard's outer office who did not have gray hair.

"Buddy? Come on in. How are you, son?"

"Fine, sir."

"You look fit, as always. Everything right at home? How's your father?"

Buddy took his time answering. It was a trick he had learned early on, how sometimes silence was the only response that worked. He refused the secretary's offer of coffee, waited for the door to close, then said, "I'm looking for a new job."

Bernard Featherstone had an actor's mobile features, product of years on the courtroom stage. "Son, your father . . ."

"My father is not a factor. I am here looking for representation."

Bernard made a process of settling into his chair. "If you're certain that's the case . . ."

"I am. It is."

"Then there are any number of local headhunters who could handle an account executive."

"Which is why I've come to you, sir. You know I've been more than that for years."

Bernard picked up the silver pen. Perhaps it was by chance that the sunlight reflected off the surface into Buddy's eyes. But he doubted it. The man had his own methods of creating a disconcerting moment. "How old are you, Buddy?"

"Twenty-nine."

"Not yet thirty. Son, if you waited a few more years, I might—"

"You know the truth. You're probably the only one who does, outside the bank president, where I have no interest in working, and our corporate auditor, where I would die of boredom. I have tripled the company's revenue in eight years. Tripled."

Bernard must have seen that the trick with the pen wasn't working. He set it down and put away all the pretenses. "Your father's company has been going through a very hard time. Any potential employer will see you as another bitter family member running from the sinking ship."

"I landed the Lexington account."

That froze him. "When?"

"Friday night. The Helms Group is back in the green."

"Then why are you leaving?"

Buddy was ready for that as well. "It's time I receive the recognition I deserved."

Bernard had a habit of treating his words like precious gems he was reluctant to release, leaving his sentences unfinished. It gave him the chance to say a great deal that could never be either repeated or confirmed. "Perhaps I might have a word with Jack, I could . . ."

"I told you. My father is not a factor."

"But your age most certainly is. You're chasing after a job I'd have trouble landing for someone twice your age. Plus, there is the issue . . ."

"I'll never get a decent referral," Buddy finished for him. "What if I was able to bring in a major new account?"

"Not Lexington. For you to leave the firm and take a new client with you would be borderline illegal."

"I have a different group in mind. One I've been working on almost as long."

"You've been working on two potential accounts of that size?"

"The project is everything but landed."

Bernard's chair creaked as he leaned back and inspected Buddy from a different angle. "In that case I suppose I could make a few calls."

The band around his chest eased a fraction. "Thanks. A lot."

"Did you have anyone in particular you wanted me to approach?"

"Hazzard Communications is looking for a new VP."

"Your father's oldest foes?" Bernard actually looked nervous. "You can't be serious."

Buddy rose from his chair. "I'm due for a meeting with the president of that new account. If I land that deal, see if Hazzard will agree to a meeting."

San Luis Obispo stood almost equidistant between two more powerful cities representing two very different California façades. Despite the devastation caused by recent forest fires and the mudslides that followed, Santa Barbara remained a haven for coastal wealth. The largest and most successful Hollywood titans made a Santa Barbara residence their reward for getting it right.

Two hours north of San Lu stood a very different version of the California lifestyle. Santa Cruz was a hard place for even longtime residents to describe, for it showed the world too many conflicting faces. The coastal roads fronted lovely bungalows and well-tended parks and magnificent surf. The University of California, Santa Cruz, regularly produced a high-value crop of engineers and technicians. But farther inland resided a very different sort of local. Survivors of Iraq and Afghanistan shared steep-sided valleys with ancient clans who remained hostile to all outsiders, especially lawmen. Added to the mix were hothouse growers whose produce was on the reckless side of legal. Even in the daytime local police never came out here alone.

Recently a group of local movers and shakers bought up vacant land near the university and established a major new commercial park. Using state money and their own tax dollars, they brought in a new crop of high-quality, good-paying jobs.

Everything about the International Solutions headquarters shouted cutting-edge. The steel-and-glass headquarters looked like two crystal spaceships that had landed so recently the blast-zone still glistened of raw earth. Translucent tunnels connected the main buildings to a series of pods. Huge bulbous windows in the central structures showed people at work. Outlying pods contained rooms where kids made silent mayhem in a crèche, while in the cafeteria next door, their parents drank coffee and ate afternoon pastries over spreadsheets. Others worked out and swam laps in a glass gym. Still more sat around conference tables and wrote on electronic whiteboards and argued at people on massive telescreens. IS ran at such a pace that most new employees had no idea how other divisions spent their time.

The IS main entrance was staffed by a lone security guard. There was no receptionist. There were also no chairs. A few visitors clustered and talked in low, tense tones. At first, Buddy had been disconcerted by the frenetic pace and the utter absence of protocol. But with time he'd decided that he liked it. A lot.

Buddy was shown straight into a conference room. As before, the group filtered in gradually, some texting, others talking into Bluetooth headsets, two in deep discussion that continued as they filled the swivel chairs. Buddy's was the only jacket and tie in the place. A few greeted him. Most ignored him entirely. Buddy smiled at the thought of how his father would respond to such treatment. But he wasn't here for ego stroking. He was after the next rung.

When the company president entered, instantly the atmosphere shifted. Eleven different and driven people focused with one intent. Get this done and move on to the next task. Judgment was swift here, and lacerating. As Buddy knew from experience.

"All right, Helms. We're here." Mark Weathers rapped his knuckles on the tabletop, and the final two iPhones were instantly stowed. "Fire away."

Buddy took a breath and rose to his feet. It had all seemed so simple at two in the morning. Now he stood on the ledge and looked down, down, down, to the swirling waters at the bottom of the cliff. He jumped.

"This is the fourth time we've met. And I imagine most of you are assuming it's the last. Am I right?"

One of the group managed to look abashed. The others just showed him the blank faces of people ready to move on. They were all aged between late twenties and early forties. Mark Weathers, the company president, was thirty-six. Married, with two children and a third on the way. Dropped out of Stanford's physics department, where he had been working on a doctorate in quantum computing. Buddy knew the basic history of every person in the room. Five department heads, two more from sales, the rest from finance and corporate planning. The greenlight board. Here to show him the door. Unless he gave them the totally unexpected.

"Here's what we know. Basically, you don't need any product advertising. And you can generate your graphics design work in-house."

Until Buddy's fourth year with his father's company, the Helms Group had focused exclusively on advertising. All their work had been aimed at a regional clientele. Buddy had changed that, slowly, subtly, often behind his father's back, bearing the rage, swallowing the resentment when his ideas proved right. Growing the company into Internet and social media. Building new divisions for graphics design and printing. Gradually Buddy had brought everything possible in-house, lowering costs and raising profits. When more than half of the region's marketing and PR firms went belly-up in the recession, the Helms Group clung to life. Largely because of Buddy's grim determination to shove the company into a future his father despised.

The VP of sales demanded, "Then why are you here?"

"He's decided to admit we were right all along." This from a dark-haired waif of a woman, scrawny and tight and perpetually dissatisfied. Head of the IS hospital group. "Apologize for wasting our time."

Buddy waited for the chuckles to subside. "You don't need *product* advertisement. You knew this when you brought me in. What you wanted to know was, could I help draw in more business? But you're already running as fast as you can. So the question is, what do you really need?"

"Nothing you can offer," the woman replied.

"At least, not legally," the kid from games said.

"What do you really need," Buddy repeated. He knew they wanted to needle him out the door. But his father's scathing blade had left him immune. "What was the real reason why you brought me here? The itch you can't scratch in-house."

"Now he's getting personal." The kid again. "I'm out of here."

"You need three things," Buddy went on. "You need national recognition. You need to become a household name. And you need fresh blood."

The waif scoffed, "You've let a vampire in the room?"

"Your company started just ten years ago, making software for hospitals. Tying patient care directly to admin and billing. Helping with the train wreck of Medicare paperwork." Buddy began pacing in the narrow aisle between the head of the table and the empty whiteboard. "Three years ago, you branched out into other areas of the medical world. That original division has morphed into four, and you're expanding at a breathtaking pace. Now you've added a fifth division, working with pharmaceutical companies trying to maneuver through the FDA maze and bring new products to market. And you're making some progress designing software for regional doctors' offices."

"Why are we sitting here listening to stuff we already know?" the waif whined.

This time nobody responded. They weren't on Buddy's side. But they were paying attention.

"In a decade you've gone from five million to a hundred million in annual revenue. Twice you've turned down acquisitions. You're a closely held group and you intend to stay that way. You came to me asking for ideas that would help you grow in your targeted industries. But you don't *need* any help. Everyone in those areas already knows you. Either they'll do business with you or they won't. Hiring me won't change that."

Buddy stopped and counted on his fingers. "National recognition within your chosen fields. An awareness of who you are by the greater public. And more people. The third issue is by far your most desperate need. You require highly trained software designers. But there aren't any. The shortage is national. The situation is dire. Without more software designers you can't grow. You can find lower-skilled staff. But the artists who create the preliminary design are just not out there. You will have to steal them from other companies. The problem is, most of them are in the Silicon Valley, and they don't want to move to Santa Cruz. They see this as a backwater region. Anybody who comes here risks never having the chance to return. Plus, they don't think there is the creative energy here, the cutting-edge potential. So even if you offer the same money, and even though that income would go much further here, they won't come."

The waif had a very unpleasant voice, like a low-pitched dentist's drill. "He's still telling us things we already . . ."

She stopped because Mark Weathers raised his hand. He was not just the company's CEO. Mark was the company star. Through his vision and leadership, every person in this room was on track to become rich. Weathers said, "Go on."

"What if there was the possibility of meeting all three goals with the same campaign? Raise your profile in the industry, make you a household name, and draw in the personnel you desperately need."

"We won't do a national television campaign," Weathers replied firmly. "It doesn't pencil out."

"What if you could do it for the cost of a standard *regional* campaign?"

"That's impossible," the waif declared. "It can't be done. What, you think you can waltz in here and . . ."

This time, it was the VP of sales who glared her to a sullen silence.

Buddy went on, "Back to the personnel issue. What is the one thing you hear most about this place? The one response they won't say to your face, but you know they're thinking. Santa Cruz and the IS focus on medical software have one thing in common. They both aren't . . ."

"Sexy." The oldest of the division heads gave the answer Buddy had been hoping for. "We aren't sexy enough."

"So my job," Buddy said, hard-pressed not to run around the table and hug the guy, "is to change their mind. Show them that they're wrong."

Five of them asked, "How?"

"One question before I answer that. How much does a top software designer make? I don't mean a designer who's moved over to run a division. I mean the artist at the table. The person who can create the totally new concept out of thin air."

Mark Weathers answered, "Two hundred thou. Two twenty-five tops."

"Okay, so we design a contest. We put together a campaign,

challenging the nation's top designers to come up with a totally new algorithm."

The waif scoffed, "You don't even know what an algorithm is."

"An algorithm," Buddy replied, "is the structure through which a step-by-step procedure is mathematically defined. It is a system of moving from an initial state and set of inputs to a desired output. It contains a finite set of well-defined successive states that can be logically followed to obtain the preferred outcome."

"There's no way you can make an algorithm sexy," the VP declared.

"Or turn this into a national campaign," the kid agreed.

"What if," Buddy replied, "the contest is to create the world's first *dating* algorithm?"

"Send this guy down the trapdoor." The kid hit a mock buzzer. "Dating agencies. Zillions of them."

"Not *finding* a date. A *dating* algorithm. Design the nerds' ideal answer to cold sweats. How to handle the opposite sex, expressed in mathematical terms. If *a*, then *b*. Right up to . . ."

The kid hit the invisible buzzer again, but this time it was to say, "Bingo."

Mark Weathers asked, "You like this?"

"You kidding? Somebody's going to design a system for me never to fail with a lady again? I'd pay real money."

"You won't have to," Buddy said. "But it's a nice thought."

He had intentionally not brought in any graphics. He had started several PowerPoint presentations, then discarded them as a bad idea. Now he was glad he had done so. The designers were smiling, their gazes aimed forward and beyond where he stood, filling the empty whiteboard themselves.

"We start small," Buddy said. "Quiet at first. Internet only. Let word filter out by 'Nerd Express.' A contest to design the perfect algorithm for handling the opposite sex. We nudge things along. Then six months in, *boom*. We go national."

Mark asked the question Buddy had been hoping for. "How much? The prize, I mean."

"One million dollars. Enough to create a buzz." Buddy waited, then added, "But there's a catch. The other part of first prize is a two-year employment contract. And the two go together. No work, no pay."

The head of marketing smiled. "We can factor in the additional sum as advertising."

"We'll be deluged with nutcases," the waif moaned.

"So what?" This from the kid. "We're not after an actual winner, right? I mean, we already *know* the people we want for this gig."

Mark Weathers picked it up. "What we want is to get people talking."

The kid was nodding with his entire body. "Get them to re-think who we are, and why we love it here."

"Which they will," the VP said.

"And here is your slogan," Buddy said. "International Solutions. We define sexy. Wherever we land."

Mark Weathers led by consensus. It was another thing Buddy admired about this guy. He asked his group, "You like this?"

"A lot." This from the head of sales. "Sign this guy up. We've found ourselves a winner."

Their chief checked the table and received nods, even from the reluctant waif. "Thanks, gang. We're done here." Mark rose from his chair. "Buddy, let's walk and talk."

Mark Weathers led him outside. A first. The company president looked even younger than his years. Even so, he carried himself with the gravity of a man whose turnover was skyrocketing, and who now employed close to four hundred highly qualified people. Mark stopped in the middle of the front walk and said, "We like you. We don't like your company."

It was the man's way to be blunt to the point of rudeness, Buddy knew, but it still caught him off guard. He was sorting through a whole host of possible responses when Mark went on, "We want you to come work for us."

"I don't know the first thing about programming."

"But you know marketing. We don't. Up to now, we've done without that skill set. But everything you said today was correct. We are growing. We need national recognition and we don't want to pay for it. Your campaign is the answer."

"You can get that without hiring me."

"You're trying to talk yourself out of a job even before you hear what we're offering?"

"Sorry. No."

"Your own division, for a start."

"I can hire my own team?"

"With my approval, of course. And you'll be wise to get input from our VP of sales. But it's your boat. You rock it how you want."

A wide screen of oaks and California pines shielded them from their neighbors. The sky was gray with the arrival of yet another spring storm. "What if I don't measure up?"

"You think you're the only one who does research? You checked me out, right?"

"I researched everyone at the table."

Mark liked that enough to smile. "So tell me why I left Stanford."

"You were bored. You wanted to do more than make a tiny impact in a new field, moving at a scientist's gradual pace. You wanted to *invent* the field. To do that, you had to go corporate."

"I'm still trying to find the next way forward. Enter another new field."

Buddy nodded, both because it was exactly how he saw Mark Weathers, and because he appreciated the frankness. "You will."

"So I checked you out as well. I know you're responsible for much of the Helms Group's recent growth. I know your father doesn't credit you like he should. I know you work the kind of hours I expect from my team."

"That's why you brought me in, isn't it? You never were after an advertising campaign."

"You want the job, it's yours." Mark seemed pleased that he had caught Buddy flat-footed, and patted him on the shoulder. "Only don't take too long deciding. We want to get this idea of yours up and running."

Chapter 5

Kimberly woke before dawn to the sound of her ex-husband's voice. It wasn't a dream, not really. Nor did it carry all the baggage that used to cling long after she had risen and washed her face and done her best to start another day.

On this Monday morning the voice had sounded so vivid she sat up in a panic, not clear on where she was, or why. She rose and walked to the front window, and looked out over the rain-swept lawn and the jacaranda trees that Preston assured her would bloom in less than two months. She stood there, hugging herself, chilled from the cold emanating through the glass. But she didn't want to go back to bed. So she pulled a rocker over and wrapped herself in the quilt. The rocker gave off a gentle noise as she moved, almost like it was humming. Over to the east the first faint light of a new day defied the passing storm. If only it could be that way for her.

The front door clicked, and Kimberly knew Preston had left for morning mass, something he tried to do several times a week. She rocked and let herself remember the sound of Jason's voice. And those awful days when she had learned Jason was not hers for life.

Jason had sounded so surprised when she finally confronted him, as though it was Kimberly's fault for trusting him. How could she not have known how he felt about her roommate? All the time they had spent together, all the laughter, how could Kimberly have possibly missed the fact that he had been head over heels in love with the woman? That was what she remembered now. The affronted way he spoke those words. All the times they laughed together. As though that was enough to explain his infidelity.

Kimberly made herself a bath and soaked until she heard Preston return. She toweled off and dressed and descended the stairs. Preston had bought this splendid old house in an estate sale. The place was in desperate need of renovation, which was why Preston could afford it. The street was lined by similar homes, all dating from the 1930s and 1940s. The central staircase was made for grand entrances, with carved banisters and polished cherrywood stairs. Preston complained constantly over how the stairwell took up a grand total of eight hundred square feet, what with the downstairs landing and the upstairs veranda-style hall. She entered the kitchen and asked, "Why aren't you already at the office?"

"My first appointment isn't until eleven, and I wanted to welcome you to your new home." He pulled a second mug from the cabinet. "I heard the rocker going at some ghastly hour."

"Jason came calling."

He poured her a coffee. "How on earth did he track you down?"

And that was it. Preston would not say more unless she wanted, which she most definitely did not. So she said, "I think you secretly love that staircase."

"Well, there certainly is a lot to love."

"I can see you twenty years from now. You'll be teaching at

the local university. Your students will cluster in the foyer for some social function they all dread. You'll serve them a truly appalling wine. Probably something out of a box with a plastic spigot. They'll pretend to love it."

"They better." He spooned blueberries over the top of his granola. He did not offer her any, because she never ate breakfast. "One peep of complaint and I'll hack their grades in half."

"Your kids will be upstairs throwing fluffy animals through the railing."

"How many?"

"Three. Two boys and a little angel who stole your heart the minute she opened her eyes."

"The boys are a trial, I suppose."

"Completely awful. But your wife loves them because they look like you."

"And where are you while this is happening?"

"I'll be the old maid sleeping in the renovated garden shed out back. Three chocolate Labs trained to attack Jason whenever he shows up."

"I'd be worried," he said around a mouthful of berries and cereal. "But I happen to be a trained professional. I've spent years learning the difference between a serious pathological issue and a morning dose of self-pity. Plus, there's the undeniable fact that my only cousin happens to be drop-dead gorgeous."

"Stop right there."

"A stunner. Total babe. Stops traffic in neighboring zip codes. The local California lads will be rioting in a matter of weeks."

"This is your last and final warning."

The silence held as they walked to the center. Proximity to his job was part of why Preston had selected the house and the neighborhood. He loathed commuting. Preston loved cars too much to turn driving into a daily chore. The morning walk was nine city blocks, just under a mile. She knew from the half smile

on his face that Preston was just waiting for her to say something, give him another opportunity to comment on her looks.
He was the only man who could do so these days. She disliked
the idea of her body and face and hair being a lure to strange men.
Like so much else, her attitude toward her looks had undergone a
drastic change.

She realized Preston was watching her. She said what was on
her mind, surprising them both. "Do you think Jason would
have left me if I had spent more time glamming up?"

He waited until they crossed the street to reply, "Jason was a
class-A loon."

"Answer my question."

"I don't think there is anything you could have done to sat-
isfy that superficial groper of women. He was the one who
lived from his looks. Did you ever think about that?"

She had, in fact. Jason's strong, masculine presence had been
part of the package. She had simply assumed it was what she
deserved. Kimberly Sturgiss. Beautiful and intelligent and capable of overcoming her hard beginnings. "I should have known
better."

"You were in love."

"Maybe."

"Don't belittle your tragedy by pretending you didn't adore
the guy. The shame was, he didn't deserve you." Preston stepped
around a woman with two corgis on leashes. "Since we're on the
subject, do you want my personal opinion?"

"I know you never liked him."

"Besides that. I think Jason was frightened by you. You were
smarter. You cared more. You loved life more."

She did not deny it. "He stole that from me, too. Loving
life."

Preston bounded up the clinic's front stairs and held open
the door. "On that particular point, cousin, I'm happy to say
that you are dead wrong."

The clinic occupied a postwar building that fronted a small tree-lined park, and only showed a narrow side to the main road. The counseling project brought together the four local churches—Lutheran, Episcopal, Catholic, and the community church, which owned the structure. It smelled of fresh paint and what Kimberly desperately hoped were new beginnings.

Kimberly liked the receptionist already, an unflappable woman married to the Lutheran church's associate pastor. Shirley and her husband had spent twenty-two years as missionaries in various Central American nations, and now ran a hugely successful Spanish-language church every Saturday evening. But today her face was pinched up tight as she announced, "There's a problem. Someone is in your office. I tried to make him wait out here. But he refused."

"Why didn't you phone me?"

"I knew you'd be coming in." She lowered her voice. "It's Jack Helms."

Preston winced for them both. "Maybe I should handle this."

"No." Kimberly felt herself instantly snared by the same tension that pervaded every other square inch of the office complex. She did not do what she wanted, which was to go prep herself in the ladies' room, like she did before seeing patients in mental wards, staring at her reflection in the mirror until her game face was on. There was nothing for her to do but march straight down the hall.

Reverend Ross Burridge stood just outside her office doorway, nodding at something being said from within her office. The community church's senior pastor had a face made for television lights and sermons offered to thousands, craggy and stern and gentle all at the same time. His voice carried the sort of assurance that only came from years at the pulpit. "Ms. Sturgiss, how are you this morning?"

"Uneasy with people being in my office uninvited."

The pastor chuckled his way around any possible discomfort. "Maybe I should stay."

"No," came the response from within. "I want to talk to this woman alone."

"I'm just down the hall if you need me. Good to see you, Jack. As always." As he turned away, he cast her a hard warning glance. Saying all he needed to about the handling of church elders who were also major donors.

Kimberly entered her box-strewn office. "What can I do for you?"

Jack Helms continued to examine her box of diplomas. "Shut the door, for a start."

"It's fine as it is." She remained where she was, angled just inside the doorway, positioned so he had no chance to close it himself. "If you wish to make an appointment—"

"Young lady, I have the power to get you fired before you draw your next breath."

The words were made even more chilling by the calm manner in which he spoke. Jack Helms wore a three-piece suit of dark gray. His shoes were polished to a military shine. Kimberly had the distinct impression that everything about him was carefully processed, measured, assessed, and done with deadly intent.

When he began pacing in front of her desk, Kimberly found herself recalling her first week of private counseling. Students were assigned a mentor, who both walked them through their first patient sessions and served as their own therapists. Kimberly's mentor was a grand old man on his last year at the university, an author of numerous books and one of the leaders in their field. He had talked endlessly about establishing the four keys to successful therapy: control, distance, honesty, and harmony. But, by far, the most important of these was control.

Kimberly realized that was why the man acted as he did. Demanding to wait in her office. Ordering her about. Threatening. Pacing.

Not here, she silently replied. *Not with me.*

Her silence unnerved him enough to crack the veneer and reveal a bit of the lava within. "You will *sit down.*"

"Actually, Jack, I won't be sitting down at all."

He stopped and showed her the affront of a man in charge of his world. Every shred, every last inch. His domain. Even here. "Did you not hear a *word* I just said?"

"Most certainly. Why don't you take a chair, Jack? You look like you're carrying quite a strain."

"Stop calling me that!"

"What would you like me to say, then?"

"You will address me in the proper fashion!"

She heard doors opening up and down the hall. Footsteps approached. She swept one hand out into the hall behind her and motioned them away. "First names are proper for therapy, Jack. You can call me Kimberly."

"I'm most *certainly* not here for *therapy.*"

"Why are you here, Jack?"

"Shut that door!"

"I will consider it. If you sit down."

His response was to stalk across the room and crowd in so close, she could smell the coffee on his breath. See the blades of pale gray wrath in his eyes. But the door was still open, and the hall was not empty. Which meant he was forced to whisper his rage. "Stay away from my wife."

"Jack, I've only met Beth once. Before church on Sunday. Before my cousin went to your house for—"

"She's coming here tomorrow. I know all about your little schemes. She won't go behind my back on this, do you hear me?"

"Jack, any member of the four churches involved in this project can schedule an appointment. It's part—"

"I *forbid* it."

"I'm sorry, Jack. But you're in no position to forbid any such thing."

"We'll see about that." His sneer was the ugliest part about him. "Pack your bags, missy. You'll be on your way before sundown."

Reverend Burridge was back before Jack Helms made it to the exit. "What did he want?"

Kimberly forced herself to show a calm she most certainly did not feel. "I'm sorry. I can't discuss anything from a session."

The people crowding the hall showed various degrees of shock. "Jack Helms is coming in for *therapy*?"

"I really can't discuss it."

Kimberly excused herself and began unpacking her cartons of books. Preston waited until the hall cleared to ask, "You're sure everything's okay?"

Because it was him, she offered the one positive thought that scampered about her frantic mind. "That man actually managed to chase Jason away. I should thank him."

Preston offered the smile she needed. "Let's not go overboard here."

Preston departed, and she continued to settle into her new space. But every now and then, she found herself wracked by faint tremors, each of which were followed by a thought two words long. *Poor Buddy.*

CHAPTER 6

Buddy had scarcely pulled out of the IS Corporation's front drive when his phone rang. Bernard Featherstone demanded, "Where are you?"

"Outskirts of Santa Cruz."

"What on earth are you doing up there?"

"Exactly what I told you. Making the deal."

"And did you?"

"Sort of."

"There is no sort of anything at this level. Either you have a deal or you don't."

"What's the matter?"

"I have the president of LA's largest headhunting firm on one line. My competitor is handling a project I didn't even know about, until you dropped by. How *did* you hear about it?"

Buddy turned onto the freeway and headed south. "I've been studying the Hazzard group for years."

"Cliff Hazzard was astounded to learn I knew they were hunting for a new executive, and my competitors were incensed. Hazzard's search is apparently very hush-hush."

"Will they see me?"

"Answer my question first."

"I have a deal," Buddy replied.

"Then they will see you tomorrow at ten. They have short-listed two final candidates. I've convinced them to give you a chance."

"I also have a job offer."

"What? Who from?"

"The company I came out to make the deal with. IS Corp. They want me to become vice president of a new marketing group I would set up, staff, and then lead."

Bernard absorbed that, then declared, "This will set the cat among the pigeons. Be on time."

The second call came so close on the heels of the first, Buddy assumed Bernard was phoning back to say Hazzard Communications had come to their senses and were disinviting him. Instead, his mother asked, "Where are you now?"

"Heading south on the 101, along with a hundred thousand other cars."

"Do you have both hands on the wheel?"

"That's why they invented Bluetooth. You're coming through fourteen speakers."

"So you can talk?"

"That depends."

"On what?"

"On whether Pop put you up to this call."

"Your father is not home. I have not spoken with him since this morning." She paused, then asked, "Did you leave Jack's company?"

Buddy glanced at the radio. As though waiting for his mother to come popping out, and show she really was a genie in disguise. "How did you know?"

"Then you've finally done it." She took a long breath. "I need you and your sister to come over here."

"Mom . . ."

"What?"

"Don't ask me to go back."

"Is that what you think?" She might have laughed, but there was such a tremor to her voice he couldn't tell. "I'm leaving Jack."

Buddy drove up an exit ramp that he scarcely saw. He pulled through the light and entered a motel parking area. His leg jerked so hard, the wheels skidded to a halt.

"Did you hear what I said?"

"Yes, Mom. I heard. What's happened?"

"Dear Buddy, I know this comes as a shock. But you need to listen carefully. I have been holding my breath for as long as I can remember. Waiting for you to make your move."

"I don't understand."

"This was a decision you needed to make on your own. With no help from anybody. To realize that you were strong enough to go it alone. Out of your father's shadow. And that Jack would never, ever, give you what you needed."

Buddy did not realize he was crying until the view through his front windscreen blurred over.

"Until then, I had to be there for you," Beth went on. "The calm at the eye of your father's tempestuous fury. The voice of sanity. But that's over. Finally. At long last." Her voice turned tense, urgent. "Now I need to see if it's possible to wake your father up. He must be shocked out of his rage and his complacency. While there's still time."

"Mom . . . I don't understand . . ."

"That's not the issue just now. But you *do* need to hurry. And tell your sister to bring her own car. I have to get started on this without an instant's further delay."

CHAPTER 7

The dreams savaged Buddy all night long. It felt as though they had already arrived before he settled his head on the pillow. Soon as he shut his eyes and gave in to the severest case of exhaustion he had known in years, the dreams attacked. His father rose like some mythic beast, tall as a volcano, filled with burning wrath. All night Buddy ran and ran. But he could not get away. Not even when he rose before dawn and staggered into the kitchen. Not even when he slipped out the back door and ran into the empty starlight. The monster followed, raging and nipping at his heels. He could never get away.

Sixteen miles later, he returned sweaty and footsore. He did his calisthenics and stretched, then showered and eased into the courtyard's empty whirlpool. He leaned his head against the concrete tile and wondered over what was chasing him. He was as free as he had been in his entire life. His mother, the only draw that could ever push him to reenter the home he had fled, had spent the night in an efficiency apartment Buddy was determined to get her out of that afternoon. He had one job offer on the table. He might land another this very day. He had everything going his way. He didn't need to ever see his father again. He was free.

Buddy had experienced such nightmares many times. But always before, the beast wearing his father's face had come and gone in a flash of panic and shuddering wakefulness. Buddy had never known anything like the previous night. Buddy rubbed the place on his left shoulder, where the claws had held him down, keeping him from jerking awake, while the beast had bathed him with flames.

"Well, hey there, stranger."

He was so lost in the recollections, he had not even heard her approach. And there she was, the beauty from across the courtyard, smiling down at him while she slipped off the too-short kimono.

"Mind if I join you?"

Buddy was already moving. "It's all yours. I have to be going."

"Aw, don't let me chase you off. I won't bite." She wore a bikini as red as her lips. She had a fabulous smile. And the body to match. "You're Buddy Helms."

"How did you know?"

"I checked. I mean, a guy with your looks, always single, a girl can't be too careful these days." She smiled. "Now is the moment when you ask who I am."

"I've already named you," Buddy replied. "You're Raven."

She rewarded him with a smile that dimmed the morning. "I like that. Just the one word?"

He did his best to hold his gaze up above the level of the bubbling water. "Raven was enough."

"Like a superhero. You better be good, or Raven will make you sorry."

"Something like that."

"Are you always this serious, Buddy Helms?"

"Afraid so."

"And out of practice on the dating front, am I right?"

"Absolutely."

"Well, that will certainly be a change from the wolves my so-called friends have been setting me up with since I moved up from LA." She made changing her position into a magnet for his gaze. "I work for the local television channel. I'm what they call a wannabe talent."

"I'd watch you," Buddy said. "All night long."

Then he realized what he had said, and would have crawled under the water, except for the way she smiled. "How sweet."

"It didn't sound that way to me."

"But that's how you meant it, right? Sweet. So tell me, Buddy Helms. Why don't you have a girl?"

"I live for my work, it's the simple truth. What about you?"

"I got tired of being chased by wolves."

"I understand," Buddy said, "better than you will ever know."

The timer clicked off, the water stilled. Buddy gripped the rail and started up the steps. "I better be going."

"Go where?" She turned over in the water like she would on a bed of roses. "Go why? The only rules you need to follow are the ones you like the most. That's the modern world."

"It's not my world. It never has been."

"Then poor you, Buddy Helms." She rolled back over and closed her eyes to the dawn sky. "Be a Boy Scout and make the water froth again."

Hazzard Communications occupied a central bastion of Santa Barbara's old downtown. The moneyed LA crowd had polished Santa Barbara until it shone like an oceanfront jewel. But it was groups like Hazzard that kept the young people in town. They transformed the former sleepy bedroom community around the university into a high-tech powerhouse. Hazzard Communications was a major owner of radio stations. They also held controlling interests in regional television groups and newspapers. They specialized in small communities that other conglomerates considered second-rate or beneath notice. What the major holding groups failed to realize was, these small stations and newspapers remained highly profitable. They might generate a smaller revenue stream, but their customers remained loyal.

Hazzard modernized, they consolidated, and they kept their head down. Until the day they acquired the central coast's largest television channel, and then three weeks later saved the San Luis Obispo newspaper from bankruptcy. Both sizeable acquisitions were made for cash. Even the *Wall Street Journal* took notice of that move.

Cliff Hazzard was everything Buddy's father was not, and yet very similar just the same. Which was probably why Jack Helms had loathed the man on sight. Cliff Hazzard was bluff and hearty, and hailed from a small town between Dallas and Austin. Cliff was tall and red-faced in the manner of a man who fought against high cholesterol and even higher blood pressure. Cliff tossed heavy-handed scorn whenever he disagreed with someone, his power so great most people claimed they did not mind. He wore London-tailored suits with hand-tooled boots, and liked to think he made the best friend in the world. And the worst enemy.

Cliff resembled Buddy's father most in that he did not lead his group so much as dominate it by force of will. Beneath Hazzard's bonhomie was a fierce determination and unshakeable confidence that his opinion was the one that mattered most. He knew the way forward. Either his team got on board, or they were shown the steel tip of his boot. The streets of California commerce were littered with careers wrecked by Cliff Hazzard. But still they came, eager for the chance to work at Hazzard Communications because Cliff rewarded those who pleased him. He shared the wealth with a Texan's openhanded generosity.

The building's top two floors had been carved into a vast high-ceilinged duplex. It housed the boardroom, a private lobby, and Cliff Hazzard's inner sanctum. Buddy was ushered through gilded double doors and directed into a sitting area separated from Hazzard's desk by a hundred feet of mahogany floor and Persian carpets. Cliff Hazzard waved to him, a phone attached to his ear, his boots on the desk; three gray-suited attendants seated on the other side watched with tense expressions. Cliff boomed a few times into the receiver, then set it down and said, "Forty-five mil and not a cent higher."

"They won't budge from sixty," the senior attendant declared.

"Yeah, they just sang me that same tune. But that's my price."

"I hear they have a hedge fund interested in the whole package."

"You know what? I think they're playing the LA version of Texas hold 'em. They made sure you heard about this so-called offer. But that don't make it true."

"And if the other buyer really exists?"

"Then we fold. Either way, I'm going with the chips already on the table." He swung his boots to the floor. "We're done here. See if the lawyer fellow is ready."

The lawyer fellow was the senior partner of Santa Barbara's largest firm, and a member of the Hazzard Communications board of directors. Stanton Parrish was urbane, where Cliff was rough-hewn. But the two men held the same calculating gaze as they seated themselves across from Buddy.

Cliff asked, "How's the old man?"

"Not here," Buddy replied.

"You into cars, Buddy? Of course you are. Every kid your age is. You catch an eyeful of my new machine downstairs?"

Buddy knew the proper response was to praise the Rolls-Royce Silver Ghost parked in the fire lane directly in front of the garage elevators. But he couldn't be bothered. He had no idea why he felt so contrary. Perhaps the disturbed night. Or how the beautiful Raven's words still bounced around his brain, about there being no rules except the ones he decided to follow. What he heard himself say was "I'm not a kid."

"Your age says different. How old are you, anyway? You look about nineteen."

"If your researchers haven't already told you, I'm wasting my time."

"That's what we're trying to find out here, isn't it, boyo? Whether we're wasting time or not."

"The answer is, I'm old enough to have tripled my firm's revenue and saved the group from bankruptcy. Twice."

"Well, now. We know Helms has been growing. The question is, who's behind it? You or the old man? 'Cause I got to tell you, I don't need somebody else's puppet."

"No," Buddy replied. "You've got enough of those already."

A predatory gleam entered the man's green eyes. "Name one."

"The head of your advertising group. He's been riding your coattails since you acquired his firm four years ago."

"They've made a profit every year," Cliff shot back.

"Only because you discount your advertising space in print and on air. If he'd even half tried, he could have parlayed his position into a domination of the regional market. But he's fat and happy. Which is why you're looking for a replacement."

Cliff crossed his legs, flicked an imaginary speck off his boot, and changed course. "I'm still trying to figure out who it is exactly we're talking to here. You, or your father's son."

"I'm the guy who could make this advertising group actually pull its own weight. But you already know that. What I'm trying to figure out is why you feel a need to play the bully."

"You got some mouth for a punk—"

"All right, that's enough." The lawyer spoke for the first time. "Back off, the both of you. Mr. Helms, your attitude is surprising, to say the least."

Buddy did as Stanton said, and settled back into his chair. "You're right. I apologize."

Cliff started to speak, but the lawyer halted him with an upraised hand. "Let me ask you a personal question, Mr. Helms. What is behind this head of steam you brought in here with you?"

Buddy met the CEO's agate gaze. "You are enough like my father to pull my trigger. But you're not him, and I should give you a chance. I didn't. I was wrong."

The lawyer looked at Cliff seated beside him. "Takes a man to admit he made a mistake, wouldn't you say?"

Cliff Hazzard caught the message and didn't like it. "You're not suggesting I did anything left-handed."

"No. Of course not." The lawyer's smile said it all.

Buddy found he was not finished. "There's something else. I received a job offer yesterday. When I approached Bernard and asked him to set up this meeting, I thought there was no place on earth I'd rather work than here."

Cliff didn't like that, either. "If your thinking's changed, why are we fitting you into an overpacked day?"

"It's not that. I still think I could make a hit here, and I think I'd be the best man for the job. But . . ."

Buddy found the same tight constriction wrenching at his chest as had afflicted him through the night. Only now, he was awake and could fight back. The two men must have caught some sense of his struggle, for they granted him a silence long enough for him to forge a decent breath and continue. "This is the first time I've ever even thought of working for someone other than my father. I didn't even know the other group was going to make me an offer. Now I have two possibles."

"We haven't said a thing about what you could do around here," Cliff objected.

"You're right. But still." Buddy shook his head, struggling to identify what it was that still held him in a tight grip. "It's just . . . right now I feel like I've wasted eight years of my life."

"You would have had to pay your dues somewhere," the lawyer replied.

"Sure, okay. But it would have been on my terms. No, that's not . . . I could have seen what I could do without relying on my father's name."

The lawyer glanced at his CEO, but Cliff had leaned back as well, his expression guarded. The hunter was taking aim.

Stanton Parrish turned back and asked, "What changed?"

"Bringing in the Lexington account."

"You did that on your own?"

"Me and my team. My father didn't know anything about it until I dropped off the paperwork Friday night."

"How many are in your team?"

"Nine, plus two secretaries."

"They loyal to you?"

"And I to them. If you take me, you take them."

Cliff grumbled, "I have all final say on hiring and firing."

Buddy looked at the man. Really looked. Saw the fierce combativeness and the love of the game. Cliff Hazzard was indeed very much like his father. And at the same time, very different. "I'll have to think about that."

"What's that supposed to mean?"

"Before we met, I had planned to parlay this other offer into a demand that my division be completely independent. Under my authority alone. Your only choice would be to hire or fire me."

Cliff's face turned thunderous, but again the lawyer halted him with a slight gesture. Another major difference between the two leaders. Stanton asked a second time, "What changed?"

"Sitting here. Needing to look beyond the fences I've raised. If I trust you, and if I am loyal to you, then I need to think carefully about which in-house battles are worth fighting."

The two men gave that a long moment. Finally Cliff said, "So, why don't you tell us how you'd run this gig."

CHAPTER 8

The rooming house where Beth Helms now resided stood in what once had been the most genteel neighborhood of old San Luis Obispo. Now it was only a step or so away from being seriously seedy. In an effort to keep the city's bad sections from creeping any closer, police cars rolled past on a regular basis. The brick exterior was framed by granite that had been carted in by ox wagon, a trek over roadless frontier that had taken almost two months. Four generations of a local family had called the place home, until the latest lot of spendthrifts brought them to the verge of bankruptcy. When threatened with foreclosure, they carved the home up into apartments and now lived off the proceeds.

Buddy learned all this from an old man creaking on the front-porch rocker, while Buddy waited for his mother to answer the door. When Beth Helms finally appeared, Buddy declared, "We have got to get you out of here."

She addressed her first words to the old man. "Don't pay my son any mind, Josiah."

"Truth never bothered me none," the old man replied. "If I had a choice, I'd already be gone."

Beth pushed open the screen door. "Come in, dear."

Buddy entered to the smell of fresh paint and the sight of his sister sliding a roller up and down the parlor walls. Buddy said, "I thought we agreed—"

"Don't you start," his sister snapped.

"I like it here," his mother said. "I'm staying."

Carey dipped her roller in the paint and shrugged at Buddy.

The furnished apartment consisted of three rooms. The kitchen was barely large enough to hold a linoleum-topped breakfast table, the parlor was only a foot or so wider, and the bedroom was so small the queen-sized bed and scarred wardrobe forced the occupant to walk sideways around to the bathroom. The bathroom had probably not been touched since the 1950s. The fingernail-sized floor tiles were cracked and the grout turned gray with age. The place shouted genteel poverty. "Mom, you can't be serious."

Beth was already back on her knees, scouring the oven with a wire brush. "It's not your decision, son."

"Come live with me. Please."

His mother leaned back and used one wrist to swipe a strand of hair from her forehead. "Perhaps in time. But not now."

"I've got two empty bedrooms, and I'm hardly ever there."

"You have your own life. Besides, it would not be right."

Carey had stopped painting. "Why not, Mom?"

"Children, I don't expect you to understand. But I *do* expect you to mind. The whole point of this separation is to wake Jack up. He's spent almost nine years staying stubbornly blind to the changes he's gone through. For this to work, it's important that I be on my own." She raised her gloved hand. "That's all I intend to say on the subject."

Buddy went out to his car for the set of gym clothes he always carried in his trunk. The whole thing was baffling. According to his sister, his mother had rented this bizarre little apartment several months back. Which meant she had known Buddy was going to leave the Helms Group long before the thought had even entered his head.

As he returned up the wretched front stairs to where the old black man rocked and smiled at him, Buddy recalled the previous evening and his mother's quiet earthquake of a departure. Beth Helms had directed her children to carry out an assortment of cases and bags. Then she'd propped a note on the dining-room table. Dinner had been warming in the oven. The house was neat as a pin. Like she was stepping out for a bridge game.

As he set his gym bag on the bed and shut the bedroom door, his phone rang. He was tempted not to answer, but when he saw the number, he knew he had no choice. "This is Buddy."

"Cliff Hazzard. Have I caught you at a bad time?"

Buddy scanned the cramped little bedroom with the yellowed walls and the cheap dime-store light globe dangling from the ceiling. One pane of the narrow window was cracked. The flimsy curtains looked filthy. "What can I do for you, Mr. Hazzard?"

"My buddy Stanton was right, much as it pains me to say it. You weren't the only one who came into that meeting raw from hidden issues."

"Sorry, I don't understand."

"Nineteen months back, I had to fire my only son."

Buddy pushed his bag to one side and sat on the bed. The mattress bowed and the springs complained. "I didn't know."

"We kept it quiet because we had to. I caught him stealing from the company. Since I let him go, I learned he'd gotten himself hooked on prescription painkillers."

An image flashed through Buddy's mind, of Cliff Hazzard's son in full wild-man mode. Hazzard Junior had all his father's fierce passion for life, but none of his drive, and no restraint whatsoever. "I'm so sorry."

"So you waltz in here, looking like everything my son wasn't. All I could think was, it'd be just like your father to drop you in my lap like a lure."

Buddy nodded slowly. "His very own in-house spy."

"That was a terrible thing to suspect."

"Yes, it was. But it could very well have been true. It's not, by the way."

"Oh, I know that. I checked you out. Plus, the longer you talked, the clearer I saw the pain in your eyes. Saw it with a father's hard-earned wisdom. So I'm calling to apologize and to ask, are you certain there's no chance of making up with your dad?"

"There isn't. No."

"I'm sorry. For both your sakes." Cliff Hazzard's tone went from caring to brisk. "But in that case I want you to come work for me. Your team is welcome, long as they pass muster."

"Sir . . . I don't know what to say."

"Take a day or so, think on what we'd need to get you to choose us over that IS group's offer. Only don't think too long. I've got two other candidates I'll be stringing along until we shake on the deal."

When Buddy opened the bedroom door, he discovered his sister poised by the kitchen door leading to the porch. Carey watched something through the screen. His mother was nowhere to be seen. "Sis?"

Carey lifted the hand not holding the roller. She did not turn from staring at whatever lay beyond the door.

Buddy moved up alongside her, just in time to see his father step uncertainly from the car. Beth's note dangled from one hand like a summons. He did not move directly up the sidewalk. Rather, his body angled crablike toward where his wife stood on the front porch.

Jack Helms waved the note in Beth's general direction and demanded, "What's the meaning of this?"

"Don't come any farther."

The voice startled Buddy as much as his father. Beth rarely addressed her husband in anything other than a tone of warm concern. Now, however, she sounded cold as a cocked pistol. Jack blinked and angled his head, as though looking directly at his wife was as impossible as staring straight into the sun. "Don't use that tone of voice with me!"

"Stay where you are, Jack."

The old black man stopped rocking and used the front railing to draw himself erect. Silently Josiah shuffled inside his own apartment and quietly shut the door. When he was gone, Buddy's father said, "I asked you a question."

"That should be clear enough. I've left you."

"You divorce me and you won't see a dime!"

"I have no intention of divorcing you. Or asking you for anything. Or the children. I'm here because I can afford this place without help from anyone."

The words struck Jack Helms like unseen blows. "I—I don't understand a word you're saying."

"That's hardly a surprise."

"Aren't you coming back?"

"That depends on you."

"Me? What in . . ."

"There are two conditions. Meet them and I'll return. Otherwise, no."

"You don't set conditions! I'm the head of my household. *Me!* The man, the elder, the—"

"Do you want to hear the conditions or not?"

He blustered, but caved. "Oh, go ahead."

"First, you and I will enter counseling. Three times a week. Kimberly and Preston Sturgiss are both trained clinicians. I would prefer that we see a woman. I feel it would be better for us. But it's your decision. That's why I asked Preston to join us for lunch. So one of them could see you at your worst."

Buddy glanced at his sister, wanting to ask if she had known. But Carey was frozen solid. She gaped through the screen door, her mouth slightly open, her forehead creased. Like she was straining to understand words spoken in some foreign tongue.

"What do you mean 'worst'? I was having lunch!"

"Second, you will meet with each of your children. You will apologize to them and ask their forgiveness for driving them away."

"What . . . wait . . . I haven't . . . They're not . . ."

"Let me know when you decide." She turned away.

"Wait!"

"Jack, I have nothing else to say to you." She stepped inside her apartment and firmly closed the door.

CHAPTER 9

Buddy worked in the apartment bathroom. He scrubbed the grout and the basin and the bath with a wire brush. He made a mental list of all the things he wanted to change, starting with the bath's only light, a low-wattage bulb that glowed sullenly above the cracked mirror. No amount of scouring would alter the way he felt about this place. But the manner in which Beth had spoken to her husband had revealed a determination that was as startling as it was unusual. Buddy and his sister shared a confused look as he borrowed her roller and gave the bathroom walls a new coat. But neither said a word.

He drove to the local Home Depot and returned with a new box spring, mattress, shower curtain, and bathroom light fixture. Carey left to help her beau set up for a gig in Santa Barbara's premier jazz locale. Buddy showered and dressed in his street clothes and drove to his favorite local diner on Higuera Street, not far from the Farmers' Market. Whatever the local growers brought in, the restaurant cooked fresh every day. Buddy returned with a feast of turnips, stewed cabbage, lima beans, corn, hash brown casserole, green beans, snap peas, and a dozen biscuits. The old man was back on the porch when Buddy returned, and declared, "Those sacks of yours smell like my mama's Sunday dinner."

"Mine too."

"Takes me back, that does." Josiah turned back to perusing the afternoon sun filtering through the elms. "That's a mighty fine lady in there."

"She is."

"Good to know she's got family caring for her in her dark hour."

Buddy went inside, where his mother exclaimed, "You've brought enough for an army."

"You can freeze some for the days you don't feel like getting out."

She patted his arm. "You don't need to worry about me, son."

Buddy filled up a plate, and took it and a fork and napkin out to where Josiah sat rocking. He drew over a rusting metal table and asked, "What would you like to drink?"

"Water will do me just fine. Thank you kindly."

Buddy returned to the apartment and filled a glass from the spigot. When he set it down, Josiah had the plate in his lap, the napkin tucked into his washed-pale denim shirt. The old man's palsy made a trial of lifting the beans on his fork, so Buddy went back inside and returned with a spoon. Josiah exchanged utensils and said, "Your mama's done raised herself a fine young man."

"You were very kind, going inside, back when my father showed up."

"Just being neighborly, is all. Folks living cheek by jowl got to know when to get gone."

Buddy and his mother ate at the kitchen table. The room was so cramped, Buddy could have reached over and pulled items from the stove, utensils from the drawer, or milk from the fridge, all without leaving his seat. But his mother served him as if she were still in the home where she had raised them. He watched her use a scarred ladle to dish out a second helping, and found himself thinking about the kitchen in their home. It was everyone's favorite room, mostly because of how Beth Helms filled it with love. She had dried her own spices. She was always making great jars of vanilla sticks and ground clove and cinnamon, and baking the finest tarts Buddy had ever tasted. The granite countertops always gleamed, and the space above the stove had boasted a row of antique copper pots. The lights shone upon the room where Buddy had sat on the stool and eaten lemon chess pie or Bakewell tart, and dared to speak of secret dreams.

He swallowed down the lump and said, "I've been offered two jobs, Mom."

"Well, of course you have."

"There's no 'of course' about it, especially not with this region still in recovery." Buddy related the two experiences, while his mother listened with the same calm intensity she had always shown. As though her entire world had not just shifted on its axis. As though she was seated in a palace. Where she belonged.

Before he was done explaining, she declared, "I don't want you hurrying into either of those positions."

"Mom . . . these are great jobs."

"I'm sure they are. But there will be others." She rose and carried her plate to the sink. "Buddy, I want you to listen very carefully. You are in possession of a very special talent. Some people are fine musicians. My gift is parenting. Yours is business. Anybody with a decent pair of eyes will see this."

Buddy sorted through several responses. "I was going to suggest you take my town house."

"No."

"I'll move out. Don't you see? They *want* me. I'll get enough money to buy a bigger place."

"It's a very kind offer, but I can't accept."

"But *why*?"

"Because your father will blame you for my leaving him."

"Who cares what he thinks?"

"I do. And someday so will you." She returned to her seat. "Son, Jack is going to look for someone to blame. I don't want it to be you."

"He's gotten what he deserves. That's all—"

"I won't have you talking about your father like that!"

He was stung by her tone. "You're the one who left him."

"We all did. And my fervent prayer is that it will cause him to *grow.*" She planted her elbows on the table. "But for this to happen, he must first come to realize that this isolation is no one's fault but his own."

In the feeble glow of the ceiling light, the cost of the past few days were clearly evident on his mother's features. Her eyes were sunken, the skin over her cheekbones looked bruised. She was always so poised, so *perfect.* Now her hair was tied back in a halfhearted bun, one gray strand dangling over her left ear. The ordeal had left his mother looking physically spent, seriously ill. It was not like her to reveal any hint of mortality. Beth Helms was one of life's unshakeable constants. Buddy felt a hollow ache at the base of his rib cage. "Why don't you want me to take the job?"

She nodded, as though genuinely pleased with his answer. "The *job* is not the issue. I want you to make a success of your *life.*"

"Either of these jobs *defines* success."

"Does it, now? What a curious thought. If that is the truth, son, answer me this. Why are you alone? Why don't you have a girlfriend?"

The hollow ache intensified. "You know the answer to that. Shona left me."

"You can't go through life blaming others, Buddy. That's your father's greatest flaw. That, and his rage. Which I fear you have inherited as well."

"How can you say that? I *never* get angry."

"No. You don't." She rose to her feet a second time, only now something about the way she moved suggested the transition had cost her far more than she let on. "You need to go now, son."

He rose to his feet. "Are you all right?"

"It's just a spell." She raised up on tiptoes to embrace him, though lifting her arms caused her to wince. "My big strong man."

Buddy took a step back. "I don't get you at all."

"I'm not saying don't take the job." She patted his arm. "I'm saying take time for yourself. That's all. View this moment as a gift. *A liberation.* Search out those elements of yourself that you haven't been able to see before because you've lived with such constant pressure all your days. Take time to *breathe.* Take time to *look.* And come to a fuller understanding of who you truly are."

CHAPTER 10

His mother's words stung worse because they had been so gently spoken. They sank in like barbs and did not let go. Buddy had planned to go home and work out. Instead, he drove to Shona's.

The triple whammy that had recently struck Santa Barbara wreaked most of its havoc farther south. Montecito had been particularly hard hit. The steep valleys with their centuries-old eucalyptus groves had become tinder-dry after seven years of hard drought. The forest fires had stayed mostly to the south and east, but a few of the fifty-million-dollar estates had gone up in spectacular fashion. The real devastation had come later, when the coast had been lashed by winter storms, and a decade's rainfall had arrived in just seven short weeks. Because the fires had stripped away so much of the ground cover, mudslides ripped through the town's main shopping districts, carrying homes and cars and people the three hard miles to the sea.

The northern communities like Goleta had largely been spared. The terrain here was mostly level, and the worst they had to deal with were flooded streets. Buddy took the Hollister Avenue exit, off the 101, and entered the developments ringing the newly completed Goleta Valley hospital. Shona's apartment complex was a charming mix of red brick and gray clapboard. The result was a fanciful blend that proved immensely popular with the younger crowd. He sat in the parking lot and stared at Shona's window. She had moved in three weeks after they broke up, or, rather, after she dumped him. He had never seen the apartment's interior. But in those early days, when the thought of her laced each breath with acid, he had often parked in this space and hunted the dark edges for some way to make it better.

Buddy rose from the car, wishing he had the strength to dismiss his mother's words as dead wrong. Climbing the stairs left him breathless from a mix of old pain and yearnings he had long pretended no longer touched him.

Shona's voice answered from inside. It was muffled, and he could not catch the words. But the tone was enough to cause his heart to hammer. She opened the door, and the half-formed smile slipped away. "Buddy."

"Hello, Shona."

"Now isn't a good time."

"I understand. I just wanted to ask you one question."

Shona's roommate and best friend appeared in the alcove connecting the kitchen to the living/dining area. She spotted Buddy, and her face flickered with emotions, none of them welcome. "Everything all right, Shona?"

The words were enough for his former love to step outside. The apartment entrances fronted an open-plan landing, with whitewashed railings that overlooked a central lake. "What do you want?"

There was no welcome to her voice, no curiosity. Precisely the sound he recalled from the time of endings. He had begged; she had gradually moved from gentle to iron hard. There was no going back. She was done with him. The tone said it all. Then and now.

He had rehearsed the words the entire way over. But now that he was here, they sounded feeble. "I'm going through some major transitions. I want to get it right. I need to ask why you left me. Not what we talked about. There was so much then, and a lot of it I couldn't hear. All I could think at the time was, we never argued, we hadn't—"

"Don't, Buddy."

"Sorry."

"You were always being sorry."

"That's the reason?"

"Of course not." She wrapped her arms in tight around her middle and turned to the railing and the waters. The grandmother who had raised her had been full-blooded Cherokee, and Shona's features were a stunning mix of Anglo and Native American. Copper-blond hair, high cheekbones, permanent tan, hazel eyes that carried a heard-earned wisdom. She was a physical therapist, and like most of these apartment dwellers worked at the sprawling new health complex. "Your father disapproved of me."

"Get in line."

The simmering coals of old anger resurfaced. "He never said your blood was tainted, though, did he?"

Buddy started to ask how that could have caused her to break up, and realized at some deeper level that it was the wrong thing to say. She was circling around something, and he wanted to hear what it was. So he held back. Hard as it was, with his entire being drawn by the magnetic power of the heart he would never be able to cherish. His voice sounded raw from the strain as he added, "My mother thought you were great."

"How is Beth?"

He sorted through a whole host of responses. "Wise as ever."

She nodded. Took a breath. Released it. Another. "I have no idea who you are."

"We were together over two years."

"That's right, Buddy. We were." She met his gaze with a fire that had attracted him from the very first moment. "And the problem is, I don't think you know, either. So, how could I?"

He felt as though she had punched him in the gut. "I don't understand. But I'm trying to."

"Are you?"

"Yes." It was his turn to breathe hard. "I've left the firm."

"That's good, Buddy. You needed to." She wrapped her arms tighter still. "You also need to go now."

"Thank you, Shona. For talking with me like this."

"Always so polite, Buddy Helms." Her features hardened. "Don't come back again. I have a life. A different one. I have . . . Don't come here again, Buddy."

He nodded, the move made ponderous by the terrible weight he carried. "Good-bye, Shona."

CHAPTER 11

Beth Helms sat in the counseling offices' waiting room and tried not to fidget. She saw how various staffers glanced nervously in her direction. People were unsettled by the turn of events. Beth Helms had made an appointment with their new therapist. She was here looking for help.

She found herself thinking back to her days before Jack. It was an indulgence she almost never permitted herself. But she knew what awaited her down the hall, inside the room with the door closed against the world. In a place meant to dissolve all the shields she used to keep her secrets safe.

Her father's father had been an unschooled preacher, a charismatic Bible-thumping firebrand at the pulpit. Everywhere else, he was as gentle as a summer wind. Ransom Brant had been a Central Valley farmer, never traveled more than fifty miles from his hundred-acre spread. He had raised almonds and tree fruit and strawberries and seven kids. Beth's father had been the first of his family to ever go to college. Like a lot of country preachers of his day, Ransom was seldom paid for his troubles. He even laughed about one particular tent revival that had lasted three days, and when they passed the hat at the end, he had received a grand total of six dollars and seventy cents. Ransom claimed that given the quality of his preaching, he'd been overpaid. Everybody in Fresno County had taken pride in calling Ransom Brant their friend.

That particular afternoon, Beth found her grandfather seated on the bench that ran down the shaded side of the house, replacing worn leather from a bridle and reins. She'd rehearsed the words all the way out from town, but when the time came, she simply announced, "Jack Helms has asked me to marry him."

The paring knife hesitated momentarily, then recommenced. "Are you asking or telling?"

"Both, I suppose."

"What do you want me to say, granddaughter?"

"That you're happy, of course." When the hand kept its smooth motions, she demanded, "Aren't you?"

"I want to be. I truly do. But there's a shadow in that man. It concerns me."

"You baptized him, Granddaddy."

"That I did."

"He didn't come forward because of me. We hadn't even met."

"Oh, I know that, child. Jack Helms was chased by the same fiends that are plaguing him now."

She heard her voice go small. "I thought you'd be thrilled."

"I can see why. He's quite a catch. Handsome and smart and well-off, all those things you already know about."

His measured response was as close as Ransom Brant ever came to criticism. And it burned her from the back of her eyeballs, all the way down her throat, to the deepest core of her being. Then and now.

A voice drew her back to the day, the church, and the waiting room.

"Mrs. Helms, hello, I'm Kimberly Sturgiss. Won't you come this way?"

But when she stood up, Beth was lanced by the same pain that had afflicted most of her recent nights. As though the memory had found a way to grip an unseen blade and slice it between her ribs.

"Mrs. Helms?"

She raised her hand. Breathed. Fit the pain back where it belonged. Where she could manage. And said the first thing that came to mind. "Sorry. I let my mind wander where it shouldn't." She forced a smile. "Well, perhaps I should say, where I don't often let it."

"That's why we're here, Mrs. Helms."

Beth shook the young woman's hand and thought the same thing she had when seeing Kimberly at church, which was, the woman was far too beautiful to be a good caregiver. As she followed Kimberly down the hall, she saw how the furtive glances tracked them. Beth realized, and said, "My husband has been here, hasn't he?"

"Indeed he has." Kimberly might have smiled as she ushered Beth into her office. But her eyes flashed with remembered ire.

"What did he say?"

"Well, let's see. He insulted me. Then he forbade me to serve as your therapist. And then he promised to have me fired."

"I'm so sorry."

"For what? You are not your husband. Nor are you responsible for his actions. Won't you have a seat?"

"I was wrong."

"About what, Mrs. Helms?"

"About you. And please call me Beth." She looked around the room, took in the boxes of texts and the unhung diplomas and the woman's gaze. It reminded her of Buddy, the strength and the fragility together in an impossible mix. "I had asked Jack to join me for couple's therapy. But he's not coming, is he?"

"I have been surprised by people too often to say for certain. But if I were forced to guess, I'd say, probably not."

"Do you think it would make any difference if I made my appointments with Preston?"

"Mrs. Helms, my one contact with your husband suggests that he is threatened by the very concept of counseling. He judges. He fears judgment from others. Or from himself." Kimberly did not invite Beth to sit again. Instead, she leaned against the desk, allowing Beth to decide where she would be comfortable. "The question you need to ask yourself is, would you prefer to attend sessions with Preston?"

"No. Actually . . ."

Beth liked how Kimberly did not feel any need to press. Even when Beth remained planted in the middle of her office, staring about her, uncertain whether to sit down at all. Finally she said, "I am not certain I'm interested in therapy if Jack won't join me."

"What is it you want, Beth? Forget your husband for a second." Kimberly smiled then, but Beth had the very distinct impression that this woman had shed a great many tears of her own. "What is it you, yourself, would like most?"

She did not need to think that through. "I would like a friend. One that is mine, and mine alone."

"I understand you."

"Do you?"

"Yes, Beth. I do. I went through my own dark time four years ago. And it seemed as though all the world was forced to choose between one side of the crisis or the other."

"That's happening to me now, and I hate it."

"I did, too. What I wanted most was one person who cared enough not to need to take sides, or even think about choices. Who was just there. For me."

"Did you find someone like that?"

"I did. My cousin."

"He seems like a very nice man. Jack was rather hard on him at lunch, I'm afraid."

"Preston can take care of himself." Kimberly tilted her head slightly, so that her roan-dark hair fell over one shoulder. "I think I would like to be your friend, Beth. If that's what you meant by your comment."

"Can I ask why, since you don't know me at all?"

"I've met Jack. And I've met Buddy." She seemed to hesitate over the second name. "You have a wonderful son."

"He's so much like my grandfather." The pain in her side blossomed again, and Beth used one hand to smash it back into place. "I was worried that Buddy wouldn't realize what needed doing in time."

"In time for what?"

Beth was very tempted to tell her. Though she was drawn to this woman, Beth believed there was a certain order to such events. And it did not start here. So she said, "Buddy recently left Jack's company. He needed to make this move while he was still young enough to redefine his place in the world."

"You show a remarkable insight."

The words threatened to release the pain. Beth mashed down harder still. "It's easier to apply such ability to my children than to myself."

Kimberly watched Beth compress the flesh below her heart. "So true. Unfortunately."

"I love Jack still. Nothing has changed in that regard. But I fear he has lost his ability to love. And I blame myself, at least in part."

"You shouldn't."

"I'm not so sure." She eased herself into the nearest chair. Not so much because she felt comfortable in this place, rather she needed all her strength to speak aloud what she had buried for too long. "I have spent thirty-nine years loving Jack Helms. Much of that time was truly wonderful. But Jack has always carried shadows I don't understand. Then we went through a difficult period in my family, and my husband went off the rails. The shadows rule him now. I feel as though he's lost to me. I'd never be strong enough to do what I've done for me alone. But the children need him to be the man he once was."

Beth suddenly found herself overwhelmed by the struggle to simply not cry. She leaned over her knees, which was good, for it relieved some of the pressure in her chest. She stayed like that for a few moments, taking shallow breaths. When she straightened, the pain was gone. What was more, she felt lighter. As though the simple act of speaking had released her from unseen burdens. Only then did she realize that Kimberly had seated herself across from her.

Beth went on. "For years I thought if I worked hard enough and prayed hard enough and loved hard enough, I could change Jack. Help him grow through whatever secrets tormented him. I had the children to love and nurture. But they're gone now, and I know it's time. Jack needs to see that he's no longer in control. I'm not talking about his family, though that is true enough. I'm talking about the darkness he's always carried. Day by day its hold on my husband grows stronger."

Kimberly took her time responding. When she did, her voice had gone flat. "Where do you want to go with this?"

"Excuse me?"

"What happens now? How do you want to apply this new realization?"

Beth studied the lovely young woman seated across from her. This new companionship she had with pain offered its own bitter fruit. Perhaps she was able to see others more clearly. Or perhaps it was simply that there was so much less of Beth Helms to get in the way. The sudden realization caused her to draw in a sharp breath, which was a mistake. She spoke around the pain. "Kimberly, are we friends? I mean, truly."

The woman blinked slowly. "I'd like that. Yes."

"Then I have the impression you weren't asking about me and my own situation, were you? It was about you. You've married the wrong man, too, haven't you?"

The therapist rose from her chair, walked over, and shut her door. Beth had not even realized until that moment it was still open. Kimberly stood there, her hand on the knob, and said, "This is terrible."

"What is, being friends?"

"You were right. I didn't ask about you, the patient. I asked for me. That is so wrong. It goes against every conceivable—"

"Kimberly, come back over and sit down. Please." When she had done so, Beth went on, "Tell me what's happened."

"I married my college sweetheart. I got pregnant. He left me for my roommate and best friend. I lost the child. They're happily married and have two kids." Her voice had the detached tone of an automaton. "He left me four years ago. I thought moving down here would help me start a new life, free from my past. But here you are, my first patient, and our first session takes me right back to where—"

"I am not your patient." Beth's tone was sharp enough to draw Kimberly back. "I did not enter therapy for myself. I've known the truth for years. I am doing the best I can, the absolute best, by my husband. I'm here today for Jack. If my husband refuses to join me, why bother?"

"So you can move on." The words carried an abject forlornness. "So you can define a new future."

Beth might have laughed, had it not been for the pain in Kimberly's features. "That's a nice idea," she said gently. "Why don't we meet together and talk about that . . . a future. But not here. Somewhere else. So that you don't feel confined by what you expect to have happen here in the office."

"Now you're doing what I should. Setting boundaries."

"I've spent my entire life doing precisely that." She eased herself up in stages, but the pain did not reappear. Instead, Beth found herself needled by yet another insight. One so strange she tried to ignore it entirely.

This woman was in love with her son. Only she did not know it yet.

Kimberly walked her down the hall, through the reception area, down the stairs, and out into the cold gray day. When they were isolated from the clinic's many unseen mirrors, Kimberly said, "Everything I've heard about your son suggests that Buddy is a remarkable man."

"I'm glad you think so." Beth hugged the younger woman, then swiftly departed. Walking away was the only means at her disposal to hide the sudden tears. When Beth arrived at her car, Kimberly was still standing there. The young woman unwrapped one arm and offered a farewell wave. Beth opened her door and slipped slowly inside, breathing easy enough to almost chant the words, "Thank God. Oh, thank God."

CHAPTER 12

The sun had set by the time Buddy arrived in downtown Santa Barbara. He drove on autopilot, not so much going anywhere as avoiding his empty town house. He cruised along State Street, past the crowds spilling from restaurants and bars. He found a parking space and started walking, listening to the nighttime chatter, wondering if he had ever in his entire life felt as carefree as they sounded.

As he approached the nightclub where his sister's current lover was playing, Buddy realized he had left one crucial matter undone. He turned on his phone, and was instantly awash with shame over the number of calls from his office, nineteen spaced over the entire day. He phoned Serena at home and said, "I can explain."

"It's too late for that" his secretary replied. "Your team left frantic behind around noon."

"Pop has been on the rampage?"

"Not at all. He passed through every hour or so. He looked in your office, glanced at me, and walked away. Never spoke a word."

"I imagine it was awful."

"Jack's silence bit like acid," she agreed. "What's going to happen tomorrow?"

"I'm won't be coming in."

"Jack won't like that. At all."

Buddy did not respond.

"What do I say?" she asked.

"Nothing. Not a single thing."

"Jack went out yesterday afternoon. He said he was going to the church. When he came back, he looked ready to explode. Did he go looking for you?"

"No." Buddy debated telling her about his parents separating, then decided there was no need to add to the woman's concerns.

"When are you coming in?"

"Serena, I want you to pass on a message to the team."

"Is that your answer?"

"It's the only one I can give you right now."

"All right. My pen is poised. Fire away."

"Tell them to hold tight."

"That's all?"

"Yes."

"For how long?"

"I don't know yet. Maybe a couple of weeks. A month tops."

"You're asking them not to jump ship, is that it?"

"Exactly."

"Have you?"

"I need to talk with Pop before anyone else. I owe him . . ." Actually, Buddy decided, he didn't owe his father a thing. "Do you understand?"

"No, not really. But I suppose . . ." She hesitated, then asked, "You're not leaving us alone here, are you?"

"If I go, wherever I wind up, it will be with an open door to anyone who wants to join me."

She breathed long and steady. "Can I tell them that, too?"

"All right. Yes. But not that I've left or am leaving. You understand? This is important, Serena."

"I understand, Buddy. Listen, I heard from Lexington just before I left. They want to come in for a preliminary—"

"Put them off."

"They won't like it."

They would like hearing Buddy had left even less. But that was going to be his father's problem. A big one. "Do it, Serena. It's important."

"Well, if you put it like that. Tell me something, Buddy. Why am I smiling?"

The Soho Music Club was gaining a reputation as the premier jazz locale between LA and San Francisco. The owners had taken over a defunct department store and transformed it into a venue known for its fine acoustics and very knowledgeable audience. Recently the *LA Times* had done a piece on how the Soho Music Club was the place to hear the next hot thing.

Ricardo's band played fusion jazz. Fusion was a catchall phrase for combining jazz complexities with other popular music—rock, folk, pop, and electronic. Ricardo's group specialized in soft-rock fusion. When Buddy entered, they were wowing the crowd with their rendition of an old Al Jarreau hit. Ricardo's voice was powerful enough to lift many in the crowd to their feet and draw them forward. Buddy found a stool at the end of the bar and ordered a Coke from a passing bartender.

His sister was ensconced in a mini-balcony on the room's far side. Carey's perch held the band's mixing board and light controls. Carey had loved music since childhood. Through a string of early boyfriends, she had gained a deft hand at the mixing process. She spied Buddy and waved, then pointed at her headphones and lifted one finger, indicating she would join him soon. Ricardo had a powerful voice, and could imitate George Benson's voice-and-guitar riffs with a masterful hand. But fame had eluded him, because none of his own songs ignited the audience. It had turned him sullen. He only came out of his brooding shell when he was on stage, when the smile flashed and the dark eyes hunted. Buddy neither liked nor trusted the man. The feeling was mutual.

Soon as the set ended, young women crowded the stage. Ricardo slipped the guitar strap from his shoulder, set his instrument in the stand, and flashed a magnificent smile to the waiting throng. He laughed and he shone as he lowered himself from the thigh-high stage. Many had bought CDs from the bartender and held them out with pens for him to sign. The rest of the band faded into the shadows, heading for the ready room while Ricardo played the front man, the star.

He laughed and he flirted and he flashed with gemstone brilliance as he moved toward the balcony and Carey. She slipped the headphones from her ears and leaned across the board to smile a welcome. But Ricardo had no smile for her. The closer he came, the tighter his scowl grew. Buddy had seen this change in Ricardo before, and did not like it. When Buddy had tried to complain to his sister, Carey had shut him down. She said he didn't understand musicians, or their need to drop the stage face with the person they were closest to. She said Buddy didn't know the pressures they lived under, the strain and the fear of missing a chance that might never come. Buddy had been hearing the same litany for years. Only the faces changed.

Ricardo said something to Carey and pointed to his ears. Buddy assumed he was complaining about the balance. That same gesture was used by front men around the world to raise the level of their voices. In response Carey frowned and swept a hand over the board. Ricardo's expression darkened further, and he snapped at her. Carey lifted the clipboard, which she used to set the levels for each instrument for each song, and pointed.

Ricardo snarled. It was a feral sound that carried across the club. Buddy saw the change come over the front man. And he saw his sister's response. The weak liquid expression to her eyes, the fear.

Ricardo gripped the veranda's metal railing and fit a toe between the bars and lifted himself up. He reached across the mixing board. And slapped Carey.

Afterward, Buddy assumed he had started moving long before Ricardo raised his hand. Either that or he had discovered a way to levitate. Because he arrived at the balcony before Ricardo had time to lower his open palm.

Buddy moved at the level of sinew and bone and raw, coursing fury. There was no thought involved in the process. He was scarcely aware of his movements at all. The only emotion he could truly sense was rage. The anger he never felt. The fury he liked to think he did not even contain.

Ricardo caught a single glimpse of Buddy's arrival, enough to cringe in a shock of terror. Then Buddy lifted him and propelled him backward. Buddy wasn't precisely clear on where they were headed. He only knew that the man was done. He would never touch his sister again. Buddy was going to see to that.

Directly in front of Buddy's gaze was the horror and dread in Ricardo's eyes. Buddy carried the man by his head. Their faces were only a few inches apart. Buddy wanted the man to see what was coming. He wanted the man to be very clear that Ricardo looked straight into his own doom.

There was a rising din around him, mostly back in the direction they had come from. He was vaguely aware of someone screaming his name. Somehow Buddy managed to catapult the two of them up onto the stage. He plowed Ricardo straight through the amps. He did not even slow down when he stomped on the man's guitar and snapped the neck. He pushed through the drum set, sending the cymbals careening off like scattered coins.

Buddy stopped when he slammed Ricardo into the rear brick wall. Ricardo was beating on Buddy, kicking him as well, for Buddy held the man a few inches off the floor. Pinning him to the bricks. By his head. Buddy did not raise him high. He wanted to keep the man's eyes very close in. His fingers dug into the man's face, compressing the flesh beneath Ricardo's jaw and over his ears. The man's pomade turned Buddy's grip slick. Buddy breathed in tight rasps. Ricardo answered with the high-pitched squeals of a little girl. Buddy tightened his grip further, ready to peel the man's skull back. Study the brain of a guy who thought he could get away with striking Buddy's sister.

The only voice that could bring him back sounded to his right. Carey spoke directly into his ear. "Don't. Buddy. Please. Let. Him. Go."

Buddy felt an icy rush flood into his awareness. Drawing him back.

Carey spoke slowly. She emphasized each word. "If you hit him, you'll kill him."

Ricardo whimpered a frantic spill of words, which were mangled by Buddy's grip.

"You don't want to kill him, Buddy. It will destroy everything. Including me. Do you hear me, Buddy?"

Suddenly his limbs were captured by a violent trembling. He did not release Ricardo so much as lose the ability to keep him trapped. Ricardo spilled onto the floor, his boots striking a spasm beat on the stage floor.

"That's good, Buddy. Really good. Now back away."

Buddy allowed his sister to turn him around. The two bouncers each carried a hundred pounds more muscle than Buddy. But something in his gaze caused them to take a unified step back.

Carey led him by the hand. Through the demolished drum set, off the stage, through the silent crowd. Out the door. Into the night.

CHAPTER 13

Buddy followed his sister back to her apartment in his Jeep. Carey must have told him that she was going to drive the band's van home. She must have said that when they got there, they would load up everything of Ricardo's and then leave the van on the street. She had to have said they would then both take Buddy's Jeep to his town house, where she intended to stay until this all blew over, and she could be certain the man was well and truly gone. Buddy assumed it had been discussed. But he did not remember anything about it. His mind was filled with a faint buzzing that dismembered every thought before it was even formed.

He drove Carey to his town house and carried her cases inside and insisted she take his bedroom. When she objected, he explained that it was the only bed in the house, and in any case he often slept on the floor, so this was no hardship. Carey kissed his cheek and thanked him. Buddy found it impossible to respond, for up close the flaming imprint of Ricardo's hand was all he could see. He shut the door as swiftly as he could, hiding away the red tidal wave that swept over him.

He didn't think he would be able to sleep. But the day had been an exhausting one, and he slipped almost instantly into slumber. And just as swiftly the monstrous dream returned. All night he fought the flaming behemoth with his father's face. The tremors woke him twice. Both times he rose and paced and drank a glass of water and stared at the moon through the sliding doors. He feared when he returned to his pallet the dream would attack again. And he was right.

When he awoke at dawn, he knew what he had to do. It was as clear as notations on his electronic Day-Timer. Buddy padded into the laundry room, pulled gym clothes from the dryer, slipped out the back door, and set off.

The weather was typical for early spring. The sky was gray and the air very still, as though the day held its breath, waiting to see how Buddy managed his burdens. The temperature was in the upper forties, chilly as he set off, comfortable after the fifth mile. He knotted his windbreaker around his middle without breaking stride. His father ran with him, or, rather, the monster of Buddy's own making chased at his heels. He thought back to the night before, and accelerated through a wind sprint that lasted the better part of his twelfth mile. He returned home and moved straight into the stretching routine, trying to halt the cramps before they set in. The images flashed more readily now, blinding him to the strengthening daylight. He did not see Ricardo so much as relive the man's terror. At *him*. Buddy Helms. The man who never lost his temper. The man who had previously assumed he held no rage at all.

From there he flashed back to the conversation with Shona, and her declaration of the mystery she had carried during their time together, the enigma called Buddy Helms, what had finally caused their breakup. The realization that she had been right to leave locked him up tight; he clenched and folded over his legs, wrapping his arms around his shins, feeling the pain lance through his thighs and rise to his lower back and his shoulders and his neck. He embraced the pain as well. It was all he deserved.

"Buddy?"

He was so constricted he had to lower himself to the exercise mat. He lay there, panting and rubbing his thighs, willing his body to unclench. The lovely neighbor stood over him, offering a splendid view of the body that was almost but not quite hidden by the kimono. "Raven. Hi."

She liked hearing the name enough to pose for him, one hand on angled hip, the other cocked out like a waitress, a mug dangling from one finger. "I came over for a cup of something. I forget what."

He rose in very easy steps. "I guess I overdid it."

"Hey, I always did like a guy who doesn't know his own limits." Then she glanced beyond him, and the playful smile vanished, the musical voice flattened into a single "Oh."

Buddy looked through the sliding doors and saw his sister standing there, cradling a mug, turned slightly so the good cheek was aimed at the pair of them. Buddy stayed like that, straightening slowly, watching the day's reflection in the glass as Raven slipped down the terrace stairs and danced along the sidewalk and stepped into her home. Only then did Carey open the doors and say, "I could do a vanishing act."

"No need."

"She's very pretty."

"She is." Buddy gathered up his mat and jacket. "I don't even know her name."

"Is that how you want it?"

He slipped past her into the house. "I have no idea."

Buddy carried the phone into his bedroom. He made his call, setting in motion the action that had woken him. When he returned twenty minutes later, showered and dressed, Carey still stood by the doors. "It's very nice here."

Buddy pretended not to see the flaming cheek, the pattern of recent tears that stained her face, or the shattered gaze. "I have to go out. The house is yours. For as long as you like."

She did not nod so much as rock slowly. "Someday I might find a way to tell you just how much that means."

"Is there anything you need? Something special you'd like for dinner?"

"Whatever." She looked at him. "Will you call Mom, tell her I don't feel up to helping her today? If I do it, she'll know something's wrong."

"Sure thing. What about your work?"

"Already done." She made a process of washing her mug. "Mom warned me this would happen."

"She told you to break up with Ricardo?"

"In so many words. She said I had found the musical equivalent of what I had left home to escape from."

The benumbed feeling returned with a vengeance, as though Buddy's system responded to yet another shock by taking a giant emotional step back. He kissed his sister's wet cheek, spoke words neither of them heard, and left.

The church bordered San Lu's historic section, anchoring one corner of Mitchell Park. The stain of his father's shadow had often left Buddy wishing he could find a church he could call his own. Now, as he sat in the counseling center's waiting room, he wondered if he would ever truly belong anywhere.

"Buddy Helms?"

He lifted his gaze. The woman's smile was open and uncomplicated and totally free of all the constricting pressures Buddy carried. "I'm Preston's cousin, Kimberly. You met Preston on Sunday, right?"

"He had lunch with us."

"Sure. He mentioned that." She motioned toward the side hall. "We're ready to see you."

Kimberly Sturgiss carried herself with a model's grace, her

erect carriage suggesting a brisk confidence. She wore gray gabardine slacks that were cut to her hourglass figure and a starched white blouse. She waited by the side bookcase as Preston rose and shook his hand. Then as Buddy slipped into the chair in front of the desk, Kimberly Sturgiss seated herself in a high-backed chair near her cousin. Preston said, "It's not usual for a new patient to ask to see two therapists at the same time, Mr. Helms. Matter of fact, I've never heard of this before."

"Actually, I was hoping I might have a word with your cousin about . . ." Buddy hesitated. He was here. He had asked for this. And now he had no idea how to go on.

Preston defused the moment with a professional ease. "Kimberly is also a trained psychotherapist, which I'm happy to say I had a hand in making happen."

"More than a hand." Kimberly revealed a lovely smile. "It's all your fault."

"Don't forget Mom," he countered. "She begged me to find something to get you out of the house."

"She did no such thing." Kimberly turned to Buddy and explained, "I lost my parents when I was young. Preston's family raised me."

"We're the same age, so while we were growing up, we pretended to be twins," Preston explained.

"Preston has always been better with people than me," Kimberly said.

"Wrong again," Preston said. "And repeating it for another hundred years won't change facts."

She waved that aside. "He had decided against the priesthood and was trying to decide what to do with his life. I urged him to get a master's in counseling."

"When I applied for this job, they mentioned there was another opening, and I asked them to take Kimberly as well. Otherwise she'd have to find somebody else to finish her sentences."

She smiled at her cousin. "Something like that."

Buddy took a long breath. He had no idea how to describe his concerns, but just the same he was driven to confess. "I'm really worried about my sister. She's been through . . ."

The silence lingered for far too long. Then Kimberly offered quietly, "She's facing something that troubles you?"

The band of tension that had been wrapped about his chest eased somewhat. "Since last night."

"But this is not a new problem, is it?"

"No." He liked enormously how she could speak in synch with him, a stranger. "Only the latest version."

"Why do you think she might like to speak with me?"

"Because . . ."

"The situation has become critical?"

"I think so. And so does she."

"Why are you here on her behalf, Buddy?"

"I sort of brought the crisis out in the open. I feel responsible." He could not meet her gaze. "I don't know if I could get her to come in. I was hoping maybe you'd be willing to visit with her in my home."

"Of course . . . Buddy, I find your concern for your sister very moving." Kimberly rose to her feet. "I have a patient coming in now. Buddy, why don't we meet in the front lobby in an hour. You can call your sister, and then we'll take it from there."

"Carey doesn't want Mom to know about any of this."

"That goes without saying." Her smile seemed genuine, if a bit canted to one side. "See you in a little while."

When the door shut, Preston gave Buddy a moment, then asked, "Do you want to tell me why you wanted to see me as well?"

The night's raw acid returned and bathed his throat, making every word a struggle. "I don't know who I am."

CHAPTER 14

The day dawned gray and damp, but by midmorning it had warmed up enough for Beth to sit on the apartment house's veranda. Her secret ailment had robbed her body of its ability to withstand even a slight chill. As a result, she wore layers—wool trousers over tights, two sweaters, a coat and a scarf and a knit wool cap. She knew she looked like a bloated ball of knitting and did not care. The walls of her little apartment were drawing together, compressing her and squeezing her out into the strengthening daylight.

Beth's neighbor rose and offered the sort of honeyed greeting she had known as a child. Josiah asked if she would care to take his place in the porch's only rocker. She declined and then waited while he drew a second chair over to the wooden railing with its flaking paint. The veranda chairs were metal and rusting. They were also the same shape as those on her parent's front porch, fashioned so they bounced gently. She sat by the old black gentleman and talked in the slow cadence of bygone days. She learned he had a daughter in Boston who was a divorced mother of two and had good work providing legal aid.

He also had a son in Detroit, and on that point he grew silent, as though to say more might invite shadows into their quiet haven. He did not ask about her family or her situation. It was not done. Either she volunteered or she did not. Beth spoke about her three children with love, though her exasperation with her elder daughter came through so clearly that Josiah limited his questions to Carey and Buddy.

Beth's most intense dialogue was unspoken. She sat and worried about her husband, and how Jack would take the news that Buddy was leaving the company. She found herself checking each car that passed, hoping against futile hope that Jack would stop by. That he would change. That he would finally take the step she had spent years praying over. Look inside himself. Ask for help. Relearn the lesson of love.

"Sometimes our prayers are just not strong enough."

It took her a moment to realize the voice was not the one inside her head. She used the pain medication at night now, she had to. The hours were too long otherwise. Sometimes the voices from her dreams lingered through the morning, as though reluctant to release their claws. Then she realized Josiah had spoken those remarkable words. Beth turned and looked at him. Josiah refused to meet her gaze. He was dressed as usual in a denim shirt and jacket and wrinkled dark trousers. Beth doubted he had used an iron since his wife had died, which she knew had been six years ago. "Excuse me?"

"My boy was arrested two years back for something he most certainly did. I pledged my home to the bail bondsman. Prayed my boy would understand what I was doing, taking him at his word, that he'd change, that this was the last time he ever walked the dark path. Now I'm here." He rocked for a time. "We were born with the power of choice. Me, you, our loved ones. We got to live with the outcome of our decisions. Sometimes the best we can hope for is we took the right fork in the road, no matter how hard the journey."

She liked Josiah's sparse manner of speech. It reminded Beth of her grandfather. "I'm afraid my husband will go after Buddy. Jack has become consumed by a rage he's carried for nine long years. I fear he won't see that he is the cause for Buddy leaving the company. He will see this as a desertion."

There. It was said. And to an old dark man whom she had only known for three days. But she certainly did not want to add to Buddy's anxieties. Nor could she foist her fears on Kimberly. Not when it might unbalance the romance Beth so desperately and irrationally wanted her and Buddy to begin. Nor could she tell Carey. Beth knew something was wrong there. And she never discussed such matters with Sylvie, who had made a lifetime profession of self-absorption.

Josiah drew her back with, "Your husband has his own choices."

"My oldest daughter made a habit of peeling away Jack's veneer. Why, I'm not sure. But I think it was her way of punishing her father for never giving her the wholehearted love and support she so desperately needed. It came at a terrible time for Jack's business. He saw it as an attack when he was weakest, and drove our daughter away. Ever since then, he's been changing, and not in a good way." Beth peeled away a single fleck of paint from the chair arm. "Buddy recently quit working for his father. Finally. It's a step he should have taken long ago. But it's done now. The problem is, Jack can't make it on his own. But he refuses to admit this to his son. Even though it's a fact. Jack can't survive without Buddy's strength and wisdom and . . ."

And suddenly she was crying. She knew it would make her face swell up. Not just her eyes and her nose, either. Her entire face turned crimson and puffed up like a tear-streaked balloon when she wept.

Josiah just kept rocking. He watched the street and the cars that swept past in their soft rush, and he waited while she reknit her world. "You've done all you can."

"It's why I'm here," she sniffed. "I pray my leaving Jack will force him to look at who he has become. And come back to us."

"Sometimes that's all you have to keep you company at night. Knowing you've taken every possible step. Even when it's cost you everything. Especially then." He rocked a time, then added, "Pondering that mournful truth has often brought me as close to peace as I've known in quite a while."

She found enough comfort in the words to drift off. That was another unwanted side effect from the nighttime drugs. She was only gone the span of a few breaths, or so it seemed, but when she returned, the black man was gone. She stared at his empty rocker for a time, then softly declared, "I know what I have to do."

CHAPTER 15

The time with Preston was not a session, as far as Buddy was concerned. Rather, it felt like an excavation. Buddy talked in a disjointed fashion, going no further back than the labor he and his team had put into the Lexington project. And how his father's lack of response had launched him into one momentous change after another. Buddy described the job offers, then shifted to his mother leaving home. He described Beth's awful apartment. He related his mother's comments over dinner. The trip to see his ex-flame, and her answer to his question. The meandering walk down State Street, the nightclub, and the fight with Ricardo. Only in this telling, he allowed himself to dwell on what had turned him so numb. The fact that the temper he wanted to believe he didn't possess had been there all along. Waiting for just such a moment to explode.

Buddy could not meet Preston's eyes. He only looked across the desk when the therapist was jotting something down on his pad. The rest of the time Buddy scattered his gaze around the room, taking in the three framed diplomas—Summa Cum Laude from Columbia, Master of Divinity from Notre Dame,

Master in Clinical Psychology from Georgetown. Preston was at least two years younger than Buddy. But the man's utter presence made his age of no importance whatsoever—that, plus the fact that Buddy needed to unload. He needed it *desperately.*

By the time he approached the final issue, he was panting with the need to get it out. He dragged in a raw breath and told Preston about the nightmares. Saving the best for last.

When he was done, Buddy was spent. No twenty-five-mile marathon had ever left him so drained.

Preston tapped his pen on his pad, and took his time shaping the words. His tone was almost academic, as though he was dealing with a case study, instead of a man who shivered from the sweat that drenched his entire body. "On the face of things you have identified the core issue. You need to cast aside the persona your father has tried to cram you into. You recognize this. You have managed to move beyond your distress and take an honest look at yourself. You seek to discover who you are."

Preston swiveled his chair around and faced the side wall, as though granting Buddy the chance to study him. In profile the resemblance to Kimberly was much clearer. Preston had the same high cheekbones, the same tawny skin, the same copper tints to his dark hair. But where Kimberly was breathtakingly beautiful, Preston appeared both hyperintelligent and fragile. As though his strength of mind drained away some of the physical stamina.

He said, "When a patient comes in with identity issues, the last thing you expect to hear is an admission. They talk about the nightmares. The poor sleep. The unsettling fear. But they don't look directly at themselves. They *can't*. If they did, they'd recognize what fills their nights with dread. And yet you have declared this very thing right at the start."

He swiveled back around. Set his pad on the desk blotter. Lined up his pen beside it. All very careful and precise. A general marshaling his troops. "So here's what I'm thinking. I want to jump over all the preliminaries with you. I want to suggest that you are going to come out of this just fine. That you will take the necessary steps and come to terms with the fact that you are growing into your own man."

Buddy felt the steel band wrapped around his chest begin to ease. "That simple?"

"Well, maybe the better word here is 'direct.' I'll give you some exercises, and we'll meet and discuss them. But yes. I think we should move on to the next phase."

"I didn't even know there was one."

"In this case I think that may prove to be the most important job I perform. To help you lift your gaze." He looked straight at Buddy for the first time. "Ready?"

"I suppose . . ." He took a long breath. "Yes."

"Good. As far as the self-identity issue is concerned, I want you to take ten minutes morning and evening. Ask yourself one question. What would you like to hear other people say about you in five years' time. They are speaking the truth. They are talking about the man they love. What are they saying?"

Buddy found himself leaking tears. It wasn't the challenge. He was almost eager to begin. It was what Preston had said. The man they *loved.* As though anyone could ever . . . "Sorry."

"No apologies required." Preston was almost brisk about handing over a box of Kleenex. "Ready for round two?"

"Yes. I am."

"Okay. Here is the core issue I wrote down while I listened to you talk about this past few days." Preston stabbed a point on his ink-filled page. "Who is your team, Buddy? You spoke about them constantly. You feel a deep and abiding responsibility to them. They are *your people.* They have given you far more than the standard form of corporate allegiance, and you have responded in kind. The question I feel you need to ask yourself is, who are they? And what do you need to do for them?"

CHAPTER 16

Kimberly was there, waiting when Buddy emerged from her brother's office. She calmly greeted him with the same word as her brother. "Ready?"

"Let me call and see if Carey will speak with you." Buddy carried his phone down the church hallway. He stood by the side window. When Carey answered, he talked to the sunlight as much as his sister. He described the meeting with the two cousins, and confessed he had mostly come in about himself. "It's really helped me, even this first meeting. I'm certain this is important. I thought, maybe, you know . . ."

It was a feeble-enough attempt. Buddy expected her to refuse outright. But Carey was silent a moment, then asked, "Mom told me she was coming in to speak to the lady. What's her name?"

"Kimberly."

"Did Pop show up?"

"I didn't ask. But I can't imagine Pop would even consider therapy."

Carey was quiet a moment longer. "What's she like?"

Buddy started to turn around to see if she was listening, then decided it didn't matter. "Very nice. Very professional."

Her voice had gone very small. "I guess . . . Okay."

"We're coming now." When he cut the connection, Buddy turned to find Kimberly at the hall's far end, watching him. "Carey says yes."

"I don't have my car. I walked here from Preston's home. I'm staying with him for the time being."

"I'll drive you over, then bring you back."

Those were the last words they spoke until Buddy turned into the town-house complex. He did not mind the silence. He remained severely bruised by his own session. The challenge to look forward and define a future where people described him with love swelled his throat to the point where his breathing rasped. He did not mind the silence at all.

When he cut off the motor, Kimberly made no move to open her door. Buddy asked because he had to. "How long will you be?"

"Initial meetings are best when they don't hold to a rigid timeline." Her voice carried a flat formality. "Is that a problem?"

"I need to make an appointment." He swallowed against the tight, queasy sensation. "For later."

"I can take a taxi back."

"No. I'll wait. I want . . ." Buddy shook his head. What he wanted didn't mean a thing. "It's no problem."

"Why don't I hold us to an hour and a half max." Kimberly remained facing forward, her hands still in her lap. "I want to say something. But you may think I am interfering. It really isn't any of my business. So you would be perfectly in order to tell me to keep quiet."

Buddy felt his body harden again, preparing for her condemnation. "Say it."

"While you were relating the issues surrounding your sister's current state, I was struck by two very powerful impressions. The first was, you may want to consider going on a retreat."

"You want . . ."

She turned from her inspection of the harsh winter light. "This isn't about what I want. This is about what you may need right now."

"No, it's not that. I thought you were going to criticize me. For what I did last night."

"Professionally, I can never condone a violent response. And your explosive rage indicates underlying issues. But a man whom you distrusted physically assaulted your sister." Her gaze still held the dark light of deep disquiet. "Your sister came here for protection. Your greatest concern has been her needs. Not your own. I have the impression this is your normal state. Caring for others first."

Buddy thought back to what her brother had said. His *team*. "I guess . . ."

"But as I said, you have issues of your own. It's not my place to say more, particularly as I am about to counsel your sister. Even so, I feel compelled to speak. There is a retreat center my brother and I went to after we lost his father. I had unresolved issues of loss, and Preston . . ." She waved that away. "It's how we came to know about this region. The center is called Moondust Lake. It's located just outside the town of Miramar Bay."

"I know it."

"Going there meant the world to us."

A sense of desperate longing took hold. "Can I have the address?"

"Of course. I'll e-mail you the details."

"Give them to me now." He could almost hear the pieces fall into place. "I've got something I need to take care of when we're done. Then I'm free. Well, not free, but . . ."

She canted her head to one side. "You want to go now? Today?"

"Absolutely." The need was so fierce he could only call it hunger. "It will be my reward for what comes next."

She drew pad and pen from her purse, found the details on her phone, wrote them down, hesitated, then added something more at the bottom. Buddy only realized it was her number when he saw her blush.

As they were walking up the front stairs, Buddy thought to ask, "What was the other thing?"

"Excuse me?"

"You said you had two impressions."

"Oh. Of course." Her sudden blush returned. "That will need to wait."

"Sure. No problem." Buddy opened the door and called for his sister. He made the introductions, then phoned his office and said he was coming in later. When he set the receiver down, he could hear Carey's voice talking softly from the front room.

Buddy changed and went for another run. His feet split the road with the same precision as the images that accompanied him. An inward breath, and he was surprised anew by Kimberly's disarming gaze. He expelled the breath, and was punched all over again by the appointment to come.

When Buddy returned from the day's second run, the soft murmurs continued to filter in from the front room. He spread a towel on the office floor and stretched. He then turned on his computer and drew up information on the retreat center. The more he read, the more certain he became that this was not only right, but mandatory.

Moondust Lake Retreat Center was founded at the western border of an estate created by a Hollywood star of the 1940s and '50s. Buddy had seen any number of the actor's films. What he had not known until then was that the actor had been written off as a has-been three different times. He had lost a child to influenza and had himself come close to death after a heart attack. But three times the actor had defied the pundits and rose from the ashes. He credited his renewed success as a result of having time apart, being able to view the world from the distance and clarity this haven had offered.

Buddy booked a room, then showered and took his time dressing. His reflection grew grimmer by the minute, as though he was donning a mask as well as his severest suit. He entered the kitchen and ate a salad he didn't want. But he needed to eat. Even when every swallow merely added to the sickish lump in his gut.

The front room went silent, and the two women emerged together. Kimberly caught sight of him and stopped cold. Carey, however, understood immediately. "You're going to tell Pop?"

"It has to be done." Buddy could scarcely recognize his own voice.

"Can't you wait?"

"It would only get worse." He realized where he had heard that tone. Only always before it had emerged from the man he was going to meet. "Besides, I owe it to my team. They need to know what's happening."

His sister walked around the dining table and approached where he stood by the kitchen's central counter. Up close he could see the streaks from recent tears. Her cheeks were still damp when she kissed him. She straightened his tie and said, "The world just doesn't have enough knights in shining armor."

Her words only added to the tension and the fear. Buddy drove Kimberly back to the clinic and pulled into the lot. When he halted by the side door, she reached for the door, then looked at him and said, "You're going to tell your father you are leaving the firm."

His entire upper body rocked. Back and forth. He gripped the wheel to keep himself in place. Intact. "The only job I've ever had. The only job I thought I'd ever . . ."

She touched his arm, then drew back swiftly, as though repulsed by the tension that radiated from every cell of his body. "I hope it goes well for you."

Her concern impacted Buddy deeply. He was still searching for a response when she opened her door. He watched her rise from the car and climb the stairs and enter the offices, but she did not glance back. Then she was gone, and there was nothing for Buddy to do but move forward.

The Helms Group had never looked more severe. His father's presence emanated through the bricks, filling the air with an oppressive tension. Buddy moved on leaden legs and entered through the front doors. He found it difficult to accept that it had been just a day and a half since he had walked out. He heard someone call his name, and was almost to his father's outer office before he recognized the voice as belonging to his secretary, Serena. He did not want to turn around. He did not want to risk having his resolve shattered. But this woman could not be denied. He allowed her to catch up with him, and said, "It has to wait."

"It can't."

"Serena, I have to—"

"Will you just *listen!* I have Lexington's CEO on the line. He says either he talks to you, or he is withdrawing his offer."

"Tell him I'll call back as soon as I'm free."

"But—"

"That's how it has to be." He left her there, gaping after him, and entered his father's domain.

His father's outer office contained three desks. Two workstations held Jack Helms's PA and a junior secretary. The third had been Buddy's station for two grueling years. The desk remained unoccupied, a silent threat he confronted every time he entered his father's domain. The desk waited to swallow his days and grind his dreams to dust.

The PA had been with Jack Helms for as long as Buddy could remember. She was a severe woman, with hair clenched back so tightly her eyes rarely opened farther than slits. When Buddy entered, she spackled the area around him with a quick strike of her glittering black eyes. This was her common greeting. She had positively loathed sharing her office with him. She went through assistants every six months or so. Serena had been one of her castoffs, as had his team's other two secretaries. It was Buddy's way of ensuring loyalty.

She used the standard greeting, which was "Mr. Helms is occupied. You'll have to wait."

"Get Jack on the line. Now."

"*Mr. Helms* says you must wait . . ." Her gaze widened farther than Buddy would have thought possible. All it took was for him to stalk across the carpeted expanse and loom over her desk.

"Tell my father that Lexington is threatening to pull the plug. I have to speak with him now. Or he has to live with the consequences." Buddy tapped the desk with his knuckles. It was a tactic his father often used when riled. The act rattled the PA more than he would have thought possible. "One more thing. Helms is my name, too."

He waited until she picked up the phone, then moved to the outer doorway. He stood where his team could see him. Hoping the promise of something beyond this grim day might hold them together.

Behind him the PA announced, "Mr. Helms will see you . . ."

Buddy did not so much turn as cross half the room in a stride. She quickly amended, "You can go in now."

"Mr. Helms," he said.

She jerked her head in what might have been assent. "Yes."

Buddy took that as the admission it was. "Thank you."

Even before he was through the inner door, he regretted what he had done. There was little triumph in gaining the upper hand over a woman whose entire universe revolved around Jack Helms. Buddy started to apologize, when an unexpected voice boomed from the inner sanctum, "Young Helms."

Buddy entered his father's office and shut the door behind him. "Afternoon, Grady."

Three years back, Grady White had inherited his father's law firm and now sought to fill boots twice his own size. With Grady's father the bonhomie had been both real and very welcome. On Grady it seemed as artificial as his smile.

"You're a sight for sore eyes! How you been keeping?"

"Fine, thanks." Buddy started to seat himself. But Jack Helms had assumed a position Buddy knew all too well. His back was to the room, his gaze focused on the view out the window behind his desk. Buddy remained standing in the middle of his father's Persian carpet.

"Take a load off, why don't you."

"I'm fine here, thanks."

Jack Helms had a voice he employed when his intentions were to bully and battle and forge his way in hostile territory. Buddy knew it well. The man sounded like he gargled with road salt. "The man told you to sit."

"I heard him," Buddy replied. "And he's not in any position to give orders."

That should have been good for the explosion Buddy knew was coming. But Jack held back. Which surprised him. The man was not given to controlling his temper. Ever.

Grady chuckled wetly, as though chewing on a good joke. "So, what's up with you, Buddy?"

Grady's father had been big and robust and shrewd. Grady was small and portly and tended to waddle as he walked. His face possessed a ruddiness that Buddy suspected came from a perpetual state of high blood pressure. Grady White stayed close to Jack Helms with a lifetime's experience at sycophancy. Buddy replied, "I'm here to tender my resignation."

Grady touched the knot of his tie. "We're sorry to hear that. Aren't we, Jack?"

Jack Helms's only response was to begin pacing behind his desk.

Grady said, "But I got to warn you, old son, there's a problem. Right, Jack?"

The tiger kept searching for a way out of the cage. Free to roam and strike and devour.

Grady said, "If you leave us in the lurch, we'll be forced to sue."

"On what grounds?"

"Breach of contract and related executive duties."

Buddy laughed out loud. "That's absurd."

Grady tried his best to look affronted. "That's the law."

"*What* law?"

"The rights of a company to expect its employees to hold to the letter of their contract—"

"Stop right there. I don't *have* a contract. I never have. Isn't that right, Pop?"

"Get on with it," Jack snarled.

There was a certain satisfaction to knowing they had come together and prepped for this moment. It was hardly enough to calm Buddy's racing pulse. But it meant his father had either expected or feared that this might be the purpose behind Buddy asking for the appointment. What Buddy didn't understand was what Jack Helms could hope to gain.

Grady cleared his throat. "If you agree to stay on for another six months—"

"Not a chance."

"Mr. Helms has generously agreed—"

"I'm not staying another day. I'm gone."

"You will *shut up and listen.*"

Buddy watched his father wheel and pace and wheel again. The pain was lacerating. "No, Pop. I won't."

Jack Helms clawed the empty air between them. *"Tell him."*

Grady's glassine hair had become slicked to his dimpled scalp. "Ninety days, then."

"No."

"We will have no choice but enter suit."

"Go ahead."

Jack Helms slammed two fists onto his desk and looked at his son for the first time. "I will *crush* you."

Buddy did not meet the gaze so much as recall all the past fears, the hurts, the slights. The hopes that gradually became reduced to just grimly making it through another day. The need to run. And run. And run. Buddy breathed around the looming ache. All the wasted days.

"Buddy, really, there's no need to turn this into—"

"Stop, Grady. Just stop."

"But, man, you've really got to listen to what your father is—"

He addressed his father directly. "You need to get your corporate act together. Devise a strategy that doesn't include me. Take it to Lexington. Today. This afternoon. Because if you don't, you risk losing the business. And you know what that means. Your profits for this year will be wiped out. Everything we worked so hard . . ." Buddy realized he was finished. The sentence and the thought were as done as they ever would be. It was no longer his problem. Perhaps it never should have been in the first place.

Buddy turned away, drawn by the solitary thought that he wasn't free, not really, and never would be until the hurt went away.

"Come back here."

Buddy left the office and walked the hall, enduring the white-faced audience who gaped and searched for scorch marks as he passed. Buddy halted in front of Serena's desk. Behind him, his team clustered. He said, "The café across the street. Bring the team. Five minutes."

He walked outside. Buddy had planned to go wait in the car, but he was already finding it difficult to draw breath. Sitting in the vehicle's narrow confines would only make it worse. Buddy crossed the brown grass, away from the limp flags and his father's window. Buddy spent a long time staring at the slip of paper he drew from his pocket. Kimberly had written a number below the name of the retreat center. Buddy took that as the only invitation this particular day might hold.

She answered with a simple hello.

"This is Buddy."

"I'm glad you called. Where are you?"

"Outside my father's company."

"How did it go?"

He wanted to toss it off with false assurance. That he was fine. No gaping wounds. Still standing. Something from the expected lies of convenience. But the air was still clogged with menace he could not leave behind by simply turning his back on the building. "I have to meet with my team. They want to know what's happening. I can't lie to them. But I don't know what to say."

"Buddy . . ."

"I'm sorry, I shouldn't have called. It was wrong . . ."

"No, I'm *glad* you called. But I need to be very careful here. I can't speak to you professionally. Do you understand this? I'm not your counselor."

"I don't want you to be."

"Then tell me why you're calling."

"Because . . ." He struggled over that. "I need a friend."

"Good, Buddy. I'm glad. I want to be your friend."

"You do?"

"Yes. I do. Is that so hard to accept?"

"Today? Yes. Absolutely."

"Well, we're friends."

"Great." He took the day's first free breath. "Fantastic."

"Buddy, as a friend I urge you to be honest. Tell them what's happened and how you feel."

"They need to know what's going to happen to them *next.*"

"But you don't know that, do you?"

"No. I don't."

"Then don't lie, and don't lead them on."

"Can I say there *might* be a chance for us to move together into a new job?"

"Are you ready to commit yourself?" She gave that a moment, and when he didn't respond, she went on. "You should only tell them what you are confident about, when you are confident."

"I don't even have a passing acquaintance with the word 'confident.' Especially not today."

"Then you tell them the truth. What happened, how it went, where you are going."

"I've left my job, and what I feared would be the worst argument with my father ended up being defused by a lawyer I have never much cared for, but could hug right now."

"That will do just fine."

"Should I also mention I'm off on a retreat, because if I don't, I might explode?"

"Are you really?"

"What, the retreat? Tonight. I told you I was."

"Yes. You did." Her voice was suddenly smaller. "Will you call me when you get back?"

CHAPTER 17

The night held a metallic chill as Beth climbed the stairs to her former home. She slipped her key into the lock and was relieved to see it turn. She had been afraid Jack might have already changed the locks. She stepped inside and stopped to look around. She had done her best to create the home that fit her husband's desires. Now, seeing it through the eyes of a visitor, it all seemed so pretentious, so rigid, so carefully defined. If she were ever to return, she knew this was how she would view it. *Jack's home.* The only room that was truly hers was the kitchen. It had always gratified her that the children had felt the same, even Buddy, who was the most inept cook she had ever met. Buddy could destroy oatmeal. She had worried he might starve when he left home, and she still was uncertain how he managed to survive.

Beth followed the noise of the television into the den, the room she detested most in the house. It was all Jack. The dark leather furniture was puckered with brass tacks, and the walls were lined with hunting prints, though Jack did not hunt. He also did not drink, so the built-in liquor cabinet was crammed with trophies and plaques and photographs and awards. She was not in any of those pictures. There were also no photos of the children in this room. Beth's fourth-anniversary present from her husband had been to sit for an oil painting, which resided above the living-room mantel. She was dressed in taffeta and pearls. Looking at the painting set her teeth on edge. The children had all sat for portraits when they were four. The oils lined the dining-room walls. Since Jack had gone through his change, the children avoided looking at their own beatific smiles.

Beth stood in the doorway and watched the back of her husband's head. She knew he was aware of her. But he would sit there all night, pretending to watch the business news, ignoring her, forcing her to speak first.

Jack remained a remarkably handsome man, with craggy features and a full head of silver hair. His magnetism had dimmed somewhat, but he could still draw in the unwary. So long as they did not look too deeply into his arctic-gray eyes.

She walked over, lifted the controls, and cut off the TV.

"I was watching that."

"We need to talk."

"You've said about all you need to." When she did not move, he ordered, "Turn that back on, Beth!"

"Jack, I'm dying."

She had known the instant she had awoken on the empty veranda that this needed to be done. Perhaps she had known it before, but it had taken Josiah's softly spoken wisdom to clarify her vision. She had to do everything she possibly could, else she would not rest easy. Not that night, not for good. The old man had been wrong about one thing, though. She had no choice in the matter.

"Is this some kind of a joke?"

"No, Jack."

"Because I've got to tell you, it's not the least bit funny."

"It's not a joke."

He had been practicing the words so long, he could not simply turn them off because of her news. "You waltz out of here and leave me this cockamamie note. I follow your directions to some slum, and you won't even let me in the door. What am I supposed to say, Beth? How am I supposed to respond to such idiocy? You're acting like you've gone nuts or something. Is that why you've gotten involved with that lady at the clinic?" He aimed his finger at her. "Because I won't have you telling our secrets to some wet-nosed punk with an armful of degrees. Our family matters stay private."

She lowered herself to the stool opposite him. She didn't feel like sitting, but she knew standing over him would only make him angry. "I have cancer. It's spread."

He dropped his hand. "There's things they can do. Chemo, surgery."

"It's too late. I'm not a candidate." She settled her hands in her lap. "You were never going to come to counseling, were you?"

He showed genuine consternation. "What ever gave you the idea I'd agree to such a notion? In case you hadn't noticed, I've got a business to run. I don't have time for such twaddle."

"It's not any such thing, as you very well know. I asked you to join me in counseling because I thought it would help you hear what I have to say. But I cannot go to my grave with these words unspoken. If I must talk with you like this, I will. And I want you to listen very carefully."

Beth knew her tone was unlike anything she had ever used in his presence. She held to her gentle voice, that was the bedrock of her nature. But there was a dispassionate reserve now. She heard it herself. As though speaking of her illness granted her a remote safety from anything her husband might say or do. "Jack, it's time you came home."

Her words rocked him. She could see the shudder, though he did his best to repress it. "Where on earth do you think I am now?"

"There was a time when our home was filled with love and laughter. *Your* love, Jack. You had your moments, and I'm not saying everything was perfect. None of us are. And I'm not asking you to become someone you're not. But there is a darkness in you, there always has been. Since Sylvie started her rebellion—"

"Her rampage, you mean. That girl—"

"Stop, Jack. Just stop." Such interruptions were usually good for an eruption, but his standard rant must have been undermined by her news. "This isn't about Sylvie, and you know it. This is about you. Sylvie's rebellion opened a fissure inside your soul. She was no longer the child you wanted her to be, perhaps she never was. And this revolt created a fault line inside you. It allowed the shadows you carry to creep out and take over. It's time you conquered that part of yourself, Jack. That is my dying request. That you come back and be the man you were meant to be."

He found something in her gaze that left him so uncomfortable, he turned and stared at the empty television screen. His jaw muscles worked, but he did not speak.

Beth continued, "The reason I was hoping you'd come and meet with a professional counselor is because . . . I've watched you turn from your family, from love, from any hint of happiness. Condemnation and judgment are not replacements for love, Jack. And I worry that you have lost your ability to even say what love is."

She stopped then. There was so much else she wanted to say. But something told her she needed to hold to what was most important just then. What was vital.

Her husband muttered, "Counseling is nothing but New Age baloney."

"Preston is seminary trained, Jack. He told you that himself at lunch."

He worked on that a time, which Beth took as a very good sign. "That's what it'll take for you to come home?"

"No, Jack."

He turned back. "But your note—"

"I meant what I wrote. I love you, Jack. As much today as I ever have. But you need to bring this dark element of yourself back under control. And heal the rifts with our children." She took a breath. "Promise me you will start on this, *seriously start,* and I will come home. But you must let our Buddy go."

This time his shock could not be fully hidden away. "What?"

"Don't fight him. It's time for him to discover who he is. Away from you. Do this and I'll return."

"You think I can be held up for ransom? In case you hadn't noticed, we're standing on the brink of ruination! What kind of son leaves his father's business at a time like that?"

"He's only doing what he should have done years ago." She held up her hand. "Think carefully, Jack. Start turning away from your own dark side, rediscover the healing power of love, and let our son go with your blessing. Do that, and I'll come home. And I'll die here, as your wife. The picture you want the world to see will remain intact until the end."

"Did you not hear a word I just said, woman?" This time his rage was real. "You're as bad as your boy! You're asking me to swap one ransom demand for another!"

She rose to her feet, defeated. "Good-bye, Jack."

"I'm not done here!"

"I know." She had to clench up tight against a sudden wash of pain. Or perhaps it had been there all along, she had just been too occupied to notice. "But I am."

CHAPTER 18

Buddy's meeting with his team went better than he could possibly have hoped. There was a singular satisfaction to their wanting to go wherever he chose, and even more for their willingness to wait until he could offer specifics. Their lack of explicit questions said it all. They *trusted* him.

He left the café and headed home. Carey had spent years hidden in plain view. She was adept at showing the world a blank mask, and revealing only the segment of herself that the viewer might find pleasing. To discuss her inner world with a total stranger, well . . . Buddy pulled up in front of his town house filled with dread over what waited him inside his own front door.

Instead, Carey greeted him with a smile and a wave at the phone she held. He heard her say, "That's right. The front and back doors need new locks, and I want your man to check all the windows as well. Yes, I'll meet him with the documents you mentioned. That's fine. I'll be there." She cut the connection, walked over, kissed him on the cheek, and announced, "She's nice."

"Who, Kimberly?"

"Of course. Who else have you brought home for me to meet, other than the dark-haired vixen from down the lane? Come to think of it, they do look quite a lot alike."

Buddy walked into his bedroom and began shedding clothes. "Not inside where it counts most."

She stepped into the hallway to grant him privacy, but kept the door open so they could talk. "How did it go with Pop?"

"About like you'd expect. He raged. I talked. He threatened. I left."

"I'm sorry, Buddy. You deserve better."

"So does my team." He slipped into jeans and a sweatshirt, then dumped his satchel on the bed. "I'm going away. A retreat center north of here. Not long. Just for a couple of nights."

"Where did you hear about it?"

"From Kimberly." He waited for a rejoinder, but the hall had gone silent. Buddy ventured, "How did it go with you?"

"I'm not ready to talk about it."

"Sure."

"Maybe someday. But not yet."

"I understand."

"But it was nice. No, not nice."

Buddy zipped the satchel shut, grabbed his jacket, and came out to where his sister leaned on the wall. "Important?"

"Very."

"I'm glad." He kissed the spot where her temple met her hairline. "The place is yours."

Moondust Lake fronted the ridgeline separating it from Miramar Bay. The retreat center contained a chapel and meeting halls and a string of cabins, each with a broad veranda overlooking the still waters. The springtime forest stretched out verdant and dotted with early blossoms. The world was so silent Buddy could hear the ocean's distant murmur.

The main house rose on the lake's opposite shore, a massive

structure built to model a log cabin. Only this one was three stories tall and rimmed by a porch larger than Buddy's entire home. The actor had built it after his second heart attack, and in his will he had turned it into central California's first hospice center. His estate was large enough to ensure that no patient was ever turned away for lack of funds.

Buddy could not have asked for a finer or more fitting refuge. The day and place both seemed designed for him. Clouds gathered at sunset and formed a soothing blanket of pearl luminescence. His was the only occupied bed in a cabin designed to hold fourteen. The electric heater ticked in the corner of his little room. The retreat's eleven other guests were spread all over the place, and appeared as intent upon silence as he. They all took their meals at the same long table, but none of them spoke. Most brought books to read while eating. Buddy carried just two mostly blank pages. The headings were all he had written thus far. The first read, *What friends and loved ones will say of me in five years' time.* The second was even simpler: *The definition of my team.* Some might have considered it a harrowing experience, having no idea what to write. Buddy considered the titles a triumph. He had found a new compass heading. The first step had been taken. That night he slept deeply. The dream with his father's face did not assault him until dawn, and even then the monster's roar was muted.

The day passed in splendid solitude. He walked along forest paths and sat at his narrow window and he spent hours doing nothing whatsoever. He ate his dinner and then stood by the lake and watched the day fade. The clouds turned a magnificent shade of rose before evening took hold. When the cold began to bite through his clothes, he returned to his cabin. He slept and again confronted his father, and yet there was no fear to the dream, not even when he woke gasping. Instead, Buddy sensed that he was gradually drawing away. The change was neither instant nor easy. But it was coming. The assurance carried him through a dawn run and breakfast and departure. It was only when he rejoined the highway leading back to San Luis Obispo that he knew the first taste of uncertainty.

He did what came most natural. He turned on his phone and called Kimberly.

She answered on the first ring. "Buddy?"

"Is it a bad time?"

"I'm about to go in with a patient. Can I ring you back in fifty-five minutes?"

He liked how she said that. Not an hour. As though she, too, would be counting down the time separating them. "Absolutely."

"No, wait, wait. How was it?"

"Thank you, Kimberly. For the gift."

"That's so great." If a farewell could carry with it a hug, it was hers. "I can't wait to hear everything. Bye for now."

CHAPTER 19

The traffic congealed and left Buddy feeling trapped—that was how he put it when Kimberly phoned him back. She sat in her bright new office with the big window overlooking three ancient oaks. She faced a green wall, minty and fresh in the midday sun, and listened to a strong young man confess to weakness and fear, and felt her heart turn over with each word he spoke.

"It's ridiculous to worry about my father taking away what I found up there," he was saying. "I know it's just my response to returning to this world. I mean, my head knows it. But in my heart all I can think of is how great it was to get away, and how hard it is to come home." He paused a moment, then asked, "Does that make any sense at all?"

"Preston and I went up there to recover from the death of my second father," Kimberly replied. "I lost my parents when I was young. Preston's family took me in. His father died last year. Preston is still recovering. They were close in a way that makes me weep to think about. They were more than just father and son. They were best friends."

Buddy was silent for a time, then said slowly, "I can't imagine what that must be like."

"Preston heard about this retreat center at his seminary. He suggested we go. I went because I was in my own trapped space. My husband left me."

"Kimberly, wait. Wait. Just hold on a second."

She felt the words grow trapped in her throat. Clogged with regret that she had mentioned her own broken past. She expected Buddy to come back with some self-centered comment. Then corrected herself. Why should he say anything at all, except ask why she was talking like this. After all, he wasn't the one who had experienced that ludicrous concept on the church stairs, the message of a love she never wanted, the thought that just would not let go.

"All right. I'm taking the exit. Wait. Okay, I've pulled off the road. Now go ahead. You and Preston went up to the retreat center. When was that?"

"Nine months ago." His words registered. "You've pulled off the highway?"

"I need to concentrate. Do you want to talk about your own reasons for going?"

Of course she didn't. But this wasn't about what she wanted. The words rose like a lament she had been waiting years to sing. A plainsong of regret and loss and yearning she had trained herself to ignore. "I got married right out of university. I got pregnant. My ex left me. For my best friend. I lost the baby."

"Oh, Kimberly."

She wiped her face, and realized she was weeping. "Hold on a second." She rose from her desk and walked on unsteady legs across her office and locked her door. "All right. I'm back."

"How long ago did all this happen?"

"Almost four years. On one level I'm fine. I got my counseling degree. I've made a new life. I accepted this new job. But on another . . ."

"You're still just going through the motions."

"Preston found this retreat center and we went. It was a glorious time. A week that felt like months. For the first time since Jason walked out, I felt like maybe, just maybe, I might have a future." She opened the top right drawer and pulled out the box of tissues intended for her patients. She blew her nose and went on, recalling. "Preston accepted the job here and came down. When he left, I felt like the rug had been pulled out from under me. Everything I had thought I might claim for myself was gone again. I was back in that same dark space. Four months later, Preston told me about this position at the same clinic where he was working. I applied for this job, thinking I could move in with him and we could start rebuilding our lives. But now . . ."

"But now that you're here," Buddy finished for her, "you feel like you're trapped again. Not moving forward. Back in the cage. With no way out."

Kimberly made a fist and struck her thigh. Willing herself to stop this ridiculousness. "We were talking about you."

"We *are* talking about me. What does it mean, to go away and feel restored and find hope, then come back and worry about losing it all?"

She wrecked another tissue. "I wish I knew."

He went silent for so long she managed to regain control. Finally he said, "Before I went, your cousin said I needed to make a list of what I wanted people to say about me in five years. People I cared about, and who cared about me. Should I be talking about this with you?"

"I doubt seriously," she replied, "that there are any guidelines in all my professional texts that would possibly cover this conversation."

"All I managed to write down up there was the heading. But it still felt right. Then and now. I feel as though . . ."

"Tell me," she pleaded.

"It's not the list that is important. It's how I'm already taking a new direction. Just because I've found the right way forward doesn't mean I've arrived." He hesitated, then said, "Maybe it's the same for you. Maybe the important thing is, you know what you want."

"But I *don't*. I don't know *anything*."

"I think you do. You want to heal. You want to leave behind the bad days. You want to free yourself from the chains of pain and regret. You want a future that is yours."

She pulled out another tissue. "And so do you."

"More than anything I've wanted in my entire life."

The conversation with Kimberly left him feeling not so much prepared as able to accept the welcome he received upon arriving home. Buddy locked his car and carried his satchel up the town house's front walk, when a man rose from a battered Ford and called, "Mr. Helms, do I have that right?"

"Yes."

The man had an odd way of walking, bent slightly to one side, as though listening to a smaller person walking alongside him. He wore his clothes in clownish disarray, rumpled trousers and pale yellow shirt opened to reveal a T-shirt the same color. Poorly knotted wool tie at half-mast. The end of his belt dangled and bounced with each step. His lumpish body jiggled as he walked up and handed him the envelope and said, "Sorry, Mr. Helms. Have a nice day."

Buddy did not drop his satchel from the shock of being served. He set it down because he needed both hands to open the envelope, and he did not want to taint his home with whatever it contained.

"Buddy, why are you standing out there?"

He unfolded the bulky document, and said, "Fifty million."

Carey walked down his front steps. "What are you talking about?"

"Pop is suing me."

"Oh, Buddy." She tugged on his arm. "Come inside."

Buddy entered his home and allowed Carey to settle him on a stool at the kitchen counter. She fussed about, making him tea and a sandwich. It was something his mother would have done, offering him this comforting presence, dancing around the space in front of his eyes, reminding him that there were people who cared for him and treated his needs as important. Good people.

"I've been going about this all wrong," he said.

"What?"

"Dealing with Pop."

"There is no deal." She pointed at the envelope. "You should know that by now."

"No, what I mean . . ."

When he didn't finish, she did not press him. Carey clearly had no interest in discussing their father. "I was about to leave. Kimberly had a cancelation and invited me to come in. I thought it could be important to keep going with, you know, whatever."

The name alone was enough to draw the kitchen back into focus. "She's nice, isn't she?"

"She's more than that. She's beautiful, and she's wise." Carey glanced at her watch. "Maybe I should cancel."

"Don't even think about it."

She was already gathering up her keys and jacket. "You want to meet at Mom's after?"

"Can't. I need to do something." He decided there was no reason not to get started, and hefted his satchel and followed Carey out.

"You just got home and you're leaving again?"

He kissed his sister. "Tell Mom I'll call."

"Where are you going?"

Buddy waited until he dumped his satchel back in his car to say, "To find answers to questions I've spent my entire adult life not asking."

CHAPTER 20

Within the first ten minutes of their appointment, Kimberly knew she was going to have difficulty with this patient.

It was not that Carey was proving hard to treat. Rather, Kimberly found herself unable to look at the lady and not see her brother. Buddy was a presence inside the room, made ever clearer by how Carey continually drew him into her conversation. Kimberly disliked this sense of boundaries dissolving. And yet she could not stop her thoughts from wandering, drawn by the man who was not even there.

Carey described how she had spent the previous several hours changing the locks on her apartment, then stopped in midsentence, waved aside her own words, and said, "Man problems. Do I need to go there again?"

"Not unless you want to."

"My problems didn't start with Ricardo. And he wasn't the issue. I was."

"That's a very healthy attitude, Carey. Could we change the subject, please? There's something I need to discuss with you."

But three sentences into Kimberly's explanation as to why Carey should shift to Preston, she interrupted with, "Buddy likes you."

There was no reason why such a declaration should leave her feeling giddy. "He told you that?"

"He said you were beautiful. Inside and out. He hasn't spoken about anyone like that since Shona broke his heart."

Kimberly resisted the sudden urge to ask about the former flame, the woman whose name she now knew. "Which brings us back to the point at hand. There are any number of reasons why you should see another therapist."

"I don't want to change."

"Carey, if you stay, and if I go out with your brother . . ."

"That would be *so* great."

"I have no idea how I could respect the confidentiality issue."

"Then don't bother with it. Buddy knows more about me than anybody, except Mom. He's also better at keeping secrets. And Buddy *respects* me. Nothing you two discuss is going to change that. Do you know how special it is to be so confident about someone that they can be trusted with the darkest parts of me, and I can still be certain he will always love me? Always be there?"

"It would be very special indeed," Kimberly replied.

"Right. So tell him what you want, don't worry about what slips out." Carey had an infectious grin. "And have fun. Buddy deserves that. Fun."

"I think so, too."

Her smile slipped away. "But be careful around Pop. Word to the wise."

"Why is that, Carey?"

"Because he's a dangerous enemy." The light had gone from her face. "And that's what Buddy is now. His foe."

Kimberly resisted the sudden urge to tell Carey about her conversation with Jack Helms. She was too much a professional to cause a patient unnecessary distress. "You're saying Buddy is in danger?"

"I don't . . . Buddy has been handling Pop's attacks his entire life." She sounded like a little girl now. Resigned and helpless. "Unlike me and Sylvie."

"What do you mean?"

"I was seventeen when Sylvie left home. Buddy was nineteen, Sylvie almost twenty-one. Sylvie had been in and out of trouble, I don't know, probably since birth. Pop punished her all the time, Mom comforted, life went on, you know? By that point I was already the house turtle. The first hint of Pop going manic, and I retreated inside my shell."

Carey drew herself inward until she was seated like one of Kimberly's teenage patients. Her knees were drawn up to her chest. She stretched out the sleeves of her shapeless sweater so as to hide all but the tips of her fingernails. She hid the lower half of her face behind her thighs, like the words weren't supposed to ever be spoken, and she was afraid of what might happen. Even here.

"Buddy called it my secret life. I hated it when he said that. Like he could see inside my shell. Which I didn't want anybody being able to do. It was too dangerous."

"Was your father often, as you say, manic?"

"Before that awful summer, hardly ever. Things were mostly great in our family. My mother was a peacemaker, and whenever the storm clouds gathered, Mom always seemed to know what to do. But then Sylvie went through what Buddy called 'the change of life . . .'"

Carey's face came back into view. Her features held the abundant mix of emotions that signaled a breakthrough. On the one hand, Kimberly desperately wanted to help this young woman forge a new path. On the other, there loomed all the reasons why Carey should be seen by another professional. Before she could speak, however, Carey announced, "I've just thought of something for the first time ever."

"Do you want to tell me?"

"Pop wasn't the first to go through a dark transition. It was my sister." Carey rocked back in her seat. "Why haven't I ever seen that before?"

Kimberly felt such a sense of inner conflict she had difficulty shaping the words. "What reason for this comes to mind?"

"Because Pop is always there. The angry elephant in the room. Sylvie is a thousand miles away ... No, that isn't it." Carey frowned with her entire body, the arms wrapped around her legs clenched up as tight as her face. "Sylvie was never what you call happy. She always took a delight in getting away with things. My first clear memory of my sister is her sneaking in our bedroom window around dawn. But something happened that summer. She stopped sneaking. She ... It was like she baited Daddy. See how mad she could make him. Like she knew she was leaving, and she wanted to wreak as much havoc as she possibly could in the process."

Kimberly decided there was no reason not to be straight with this woman. "Some people with severe emotional issues seek parental connection in whatever manner they find predictable. Yes, it is possible that Sylvie recognized the dark side to your father's nature as being who she saw herself to be. He sought to hide this component of his character even from himself. Perhaps he sought to claim that it did not exist at all. Sylvie had chosen to embrace it. She saw these confrontations as the most honest way to connect with your father."

"They connected all right. All that summer and into the fall. Then Sylvie left and never came home again." Carey's face shone with the astonishment of discovery. "That was the same summer I started getting into music. Why haven't I ever thought about that until now?"

"Carey, I really—"

"And Buddy was the one who started it all. I mean, sure, I've always been into music. But Buddy used his money from a summer job to buy me a laptop and software system so I could begin mixing." Her face abruptly creased with the effort to force words through sudden tears. "He was protecting me even then. Giving me a way out. A place to hide and grow. And I've never thanked him. I never even saw it until . . ."

Kimberly had the professional's response there in her mind. She could have waited until Carey finished, then explain that in times of great stress, a natural response from young people in vulnerable emotional states was to dive into whatever offered them a sense of safe distance. She could explain that Carey's reaction was completely natural, that to acknowledge the gift or the giver risked drawing a fragment of what they sought to run from into their hiding place. Instead, Kimberly did the only thing that made any sense, which was to rise from her chair and walk around her desk and kneel beside Carey's chair and hold her and rock her and let her weep.

CHAPTER 21

Buddy took the 101 north out of San Luis Obispo. At Paso Robles he turned east on State Road 46, an older highway that cut through wine country before entering the flat Central Valley. The road's solitude formed a welcome distance to the shock over being sued for the first time in his life. The clownish man with his jiggly walk approached him over and over. Buddy was fairly certain the nightmare monster had just grown a sidekick.

He drove under the I-5 and headed east on the old State Road 41, so lost in thought that the time and the distance did not touch him. At Lemoore he took an even smaller regional highway, veined with bad repairs like an old man's nose. As he passed through Visalia, his phone rang. It was lovely to hear Kimberly's voice fill his car. "Carey told me about your father taking you to court, Buddy. I'm so sorry."

He was not going to hide away. Not with Kimberly. Not ever. "It was a shock."

"To be struck by this just as you're arriving back from the retreat, that must have been awful."

"What if this was why I went on retreat?"

"That doesn't . . . I don't understand."

He watched the thoughts coalesce in the empty two-lane ahead of him. "I went up there hoping to get a clearer sense of who I am. But nothing happened. I rested. That's all. But maybe this was exactly what I needed. A time to regroup and prepare. So I'd be ready when I got home and they attacked."

The road drilled through a series of former almond farms. The ten-year drought had rendered the trees into bone-white sculptures. Recent storms had refilled the reservoirs, and here and there a few of the trees were coming back to life. Buddy liked how Kimberly took her time responding. Finally she asked, "Where are you now?"

"West of the Sequoia National Park. I've been going about this all wrong. The first thing I do when I face a problem at work is I prepare. I am good at research. I hunt down every possible detail about the issue and the people I'm facing."

She spoke very slowly. "So now you're . . ."

"I know almost nothing about Pop's early days. I know where he's from. I know he lost his parents when he was very young. I know he was raised by his grandfather and some other nameless kin. I know he left the family farm when he was sixteen. I know he studied at UC Davis. I know he met Mom there. *And that's not enough.* I've respected his silence and his secrets. But not anymore. I feel like . . ."

Kimberly let the silence hold them for a time, then urged, "Tell me what you are thinking, Buddy. Please."

"All these years I've worked with Pop, I stayed focused on how he used to be." Buddy's thoughts formed with the slowness of frozen honey, as though he struggled for clarity against the weight of years. "But he isn't that man anymore, is he?"

Her voice carried a remarkable mixture of concern and well-honed intelligence. "Given everything I am learning about Jack from you and your family, I would surmise that your father went through a major upheaval. As a result his life has become dominated by something he refuses to acknowledge. Or perhaps recognize that it even exists."

"But it does," Buddy said. "And I haven't wanted to accept that this is the man he is now. I've wanted to imagine that somehow I could be a good-enough son to take things back to the way they once were."

He expected her to say that this wasn't his responsibility—which he knew. But this wasn't about knowing, or even accepting. For the first time in his life, Buddy felt as though he had finally come face-to-face with why he had remained working for his father for so long.

Instead, Kimberly asked, "So you are traveling . . . ?"

"I need to know who I'm dealing with here. Because the truth is, I don't know my father at all."

The town of Bennington was typical for the Sierra foothills. The main street was fronted by a tangled lace of brick and age. Decorations from some distant celebration hung forlorn and tawdry along slanted telephone posts. Half the storefronts were empty. Most of the vehicles parked down the too-silent avenue were rusty pickups. Up ahead, the road ended at the base of a wooded rise. A brown hardwood forest clung to the hillside with the same grim determination that Buddy saw mirrored on every face he passed. He walked down the street until he found the town's one surviving diner. The glass front door possessed a bell that clanged when he entered. The faces that turned his way were all old and seamed with hard luck and grueling years. The young people would gather at the fast-food joints on the outskirts of town. Or they would be gone.

"Sit wherever you like, hon. I'll be right with you." She was heavy and swayed slightly as she walked over. Her smile was both warm and weary. "Coffee?"

"Please."

"The meat loaf is dandy."

"Sounds good."

Buddy ate and felt the gazes slip over him in the polite manner of people who were unused to strangers and not inclined to make him welcome. When he was done, and he had refused the offer of a recharged mug, the waitress finally asked the question he'd been hoping for. "What brings you to these parts?"

"My father is from here."

"That so? What's his name?"

"Jack Helms."

"Don't ring a bell."

"It was some time ago."

She swung her pot in the direction of a table by the rear wall, where a group of old men clustered. "If anybody'd know your kin, it'd be them back there."

He noted how she did not bother with the questions he'd have expected anywhere else. Why Buddy had waited until he was grown to come calling. Or why his father had left and never returned. Buddy took his mug and walked back to the rear table. "I'm sorry to trouble you. My name—"

"I know who you are, boy." The man wore bifocals and a battered Dodge Ram cap. "When you walked in that door, I said to myself, 'Great heavens above. Young Jack has finally dragged his sorry carcass back home.' What's your name, boy?"

"Buddy. Buddy Helms. Jack Helms is my father."

"Had to be Jack's boy I saw. Almost like they did—whatcha call it?—them scientists making one body straight from another?"

"Cloning."

The man was all sinew and sagging skin. He used a grimy work boot to kick out the table's empty chair. "Bet you get that a lot."

"No, sir. Actually, I've never heard it before in my life."

"Go on, now."

"I've never seen a photograph of my father earlier than my parents' wedding. I don't know a thing about his early life."

"So you finally decided to come calling. See what you could dig up on your own."

"Something like that."

"Where's your old man now?"

"He and my family live in San Luis Obispo. All but my older sister, who moved north."

"San Lu's as good a place as any, I suppose, for losing a body in a crowd. Which I suspect was Jack's purpose all along."

Buddy sipped at his cold coffee and did not reply.

The talk resumed its wandering course, moving from crops to the weather to the local high-school football team. No further mention was made of the man who had left these men and their town behind. They asked Buddy no questions. Buddy sat and waited them out.

Finally the old man in bifocals rose and gestured with one arthritic hand for Buddy to follow. He shuffled across the diner, waved a vague farewell to the waitress, and headed for an ancient pickup parked at the curb. The seat smelled of oil and old sweat and the front windscreen was cracked. The truck's curved hood might once have been black, or it could have been blue. The old man's hand seemed permanently molded to fit around the plastic bulb on the gearshift emerging from the steering column. Buddy did not try for small talk, and the man did not seem to care. Whatever reasons had brought the Helms boy back home were none of his affair.

The old truck wheezed out of town, the grinding gears as loud as the motor. They took a narrow highway deep into the shadowed hills. Twenty minutes later, the old man pulled to the side of the empty road and pointed out Buddy's window. "That there's your pappy's spread. Still belongs to him, far as I know. Ain't nobody ever come asking to buy it, I can tell you that much."

A sullen stream trickled down the base of a steep-sided valley. The narrow base had once been cleared and tilled, but was now overgrown. "Where was his home?"

"Track your way up the right side. See that ledge midway up the slope?"

"I can't . . ."

"Don't matter none. Ain't nothing left but the foundation stones."

"What happened to the family?"

"Not enough bottomland is what happened. This here is what we used to call a heartbreak valley. They planted fruit trees along the creek, strawberries and such up to where the slopes grew too steep. They did well enough in years when the rains came. But a long drought wrecked their lives and killed your grandmother before Jack had his first hard-sole shoes. Your grandpappy, he held on to the farm by making apple-jack." The old man wiped a string of spittle from the edge of his mouth. "You ever tasted homemade brandy?"

"I haven't. No, sir."

"Your grandpappy had a fair hand at 'jack. Got in some bar-rels of peach and pear as well. He made his own charcoal, he sure to goodness had enough wood. He ran his mix through a charcoal filter. Smoothed out the taste. Got himself an extra twenty cents a jar. They did all right, till the revenuers came a huntin'." He pointed down the valley, his finger curved and trembling. "Them revenuers struck down both ends of the val-ley. Wasn't nowhere for your kin to go but up the slope. Jack's family chose to shoot it out. Stubborn pride and no hope make for a terrible mix. The revenuers got your grandpappy, his brother, his boy. Your pappy was the only one lived to breathe another day." The old man dropped his hand. "Heartbreak val-ley, sure enough."

They drove back into town in silence. When they pulled up in front of the diner, Buddy asked, "Any idea what happened to my father after that?"

"Your old man didn't tell you, maybe it's best you let the past stay buried."

Buddy remained where he was, and did not speak.

The man's breathing rattled his throat. "I don't know nothing for certain, understand. But I heard it enough to say it's probably true. By that time the big grower-combines out in the flatlands, over by Visalia and Hamlin, they put in together and set up canning factories all their very own. Around when your family got shot up by the revenuers, the canneries had maybe six hundred people working there. The work was steady, and for a time that was enough. But it's the way of folks when they get a little to want more. So they complained, and somebody up north sent down some organizers. The folks had good reason to complain, that's what I heard. Wasn't no easy street, working in them canning mills."

Buddy stared at the old man. "My father was a union buster."

"All I can tell you is, one day your old man was running from them revenuers and sleeping in my pappy's chicken coop. The next, he had himself a pocketful of folding money. He wasn't more than a few weeks past his seventeenth birthday. Suddenly the boy is sleeping in the town's finest boardinghouse and wearing pants with a seam you could cut yourself on."

Buddy stared out the cracked front windscreen. The pieces fit together so tightly he could almost hear the fragments click into place. The rage, the unbending determination, the righteous black-and-white perspective, the rants, the fury.

"He must've been good at whatever they had him doing. On account of how he got sent to another of their factories. Came back driving a new car. Said he was headed down to Hamlin. That was the last I ever saw of old Jack. Leaving town in the first new car I'd ever laid eyes on." He reached over. "Let me see your hands, boy."

Buddy held them out. The old man ran his thumbs down the palms and smiled. "Got Jack's size, but not much else. You ever seen the working end of a plow?"

"No, sir."

"Oh, my, yes, these here are city hands." He turned them

over and ran his thumbs over the knuckles. "Don't get in many fights, neither. Your old man, now, he was a brawler. Always did love a good fight, your Jack."

Buddy thanked the man and stepped from the car. He stood there and waved as the pickup trundled away. As far as he could tell, the old man never glanced back.

CHAPTER 22

It was the worst possible moment to have the pain overtake her. Beth had known such attacks before, but up to now they had struck in her weakest hour, just before going to bed. The tablets had become a crutch, she knew, and their effect was so pleasant she actually looked forward to them now. They came with all sorts of warnings about grave side effects. But the visiting nurse had told her flat out that Beth would not be around long enough to worry about something as inconsequential as addiction. The nurse's instructions could not have been more clear. At the first sign of pain, take the tablet. To wait only heightened the dosage required to erase the pain. But pleasant as the fog was, Beth could not abide having her thoughts grow addled. Especially now.

Even so, she knew she was going to have to take a pill. She couldn't meet her visitor standing all hunched over with one hand strung up to her side like a chicken wing. So she stopped fighting the inevitable. Then she hurried out to the veranda, where to her vast relief Josiah was in his customary position, rocking gently, watching the world sweep past their front lawn. "I need your help. I have company coming and—"

"Say no more, Beth." He pushed himself out of the rocker and shuffled toward his door. "I'll just go see to my dinner."

"Will you please hold up and listen? I have a guest coming and I'm in pain."

"I can see that. What can I do?"

"She mustn't know I've taken a pill. I need to go lie down for a while. These pills, they make me so groggy I can't think straight. I need you to come wake me when she shows up."

Josiah did not like that one bit. "What is your guest gonna think about an old black man going into your bedroom?"

"More than she will seeing me passed out."

"Why don't you just tell her?"

"Because I can't. My family doesn't know yet. Well, my husband does, but the children must be told before the world." She felt the first wave of comforting oblivion rise up inside. "Will you help me or not?"

"Well, of course I'll help. But not by me waltzing into your bedroom. I can't imagine what secrets you're trying to hide, but it can't be worse than your kin suspecting you've taken up with the likes of me."

She allowed him to take her arm. "She's not my kin. She might be someday. If my boy has the sense God gave a gnat."

"She's pretty, I take it."

"A lovely spirit inside a beautiful lady." She leaned on him more than she meant to, but just then she had no choice. "Oh, my."

"Steady, now."

"I had no idea they were so strong. Normally, I only take them at night."

"Well, at least you've stopped looking like you're gonna keel over from the pain. Now you just look ready to keel over. Anyplace you can lie down except your bedroom?"

"The sofa in the parlor might work."

"All right, here's what we're gonna do." He eased her down, then covered her with a blanket. "I'm gonna open that window just a fraction. Soon as she pulls up, I'll reach through with my cane and nudge you. How does that sound?"

"I didn't know you had a cane."

"You're not the only one hiding ailments. What is the lady driving?"

"I have no idea. But her name is Kimberly and she's tall, with long hair that's sort of black and red at the same time. She's supposed to be here around two."

"That leaves you almost an hour for a rest." He remained standing over her. "Is it bad, what ails you?"

She did not need to ask what he was talking about. "Bad as it can be, I suppose."

He hummed a sympathetic note. "You rest now. I'll stand watch."

The invitation to meet Beth Helms at her new apartment had caught Kimberly by surprise. But as she drove along the unfamiliar downtown streets, Kimberly wondered if Beth already knew what she intended to say. Which was impossible. But still. The chance to talk together away from the counseling center was a relief.

Nothing could have prepared her for the apartment building. Beth Helms was a slender, elegant woman who dressed in a timeless manner. She was quiet and still enough to fade comfortably into the scenery, which Kimberly suspected she often did. She would have looked at home in a palace.

Kimberly checked the address another time. The residence had once been stately, she supposed. Now it was one step above falling apart. The brown lawn was more dirt than grass. The front walk was cracked, the veranda's railing was more raw

wood than paint, the window frames were splintered, the roof peeling. The building would not have been out of place in Detroit.

An old black man was rising from a rocking chair before she climbed from the car. He was dressed in a flannel shirt and dark denims. Kimberly locked her car and approached. "I'm sorry to disturb you, I was told this was the address of Beth Helms."

"The lady should be along directly. Would you care to have a seat?"

The man seemed friendly enough. Even so, Kimberly hesitated climbing the stairs. "No, thank you."

The screen door closest to the stairs creaked open. "Kimberly. How wonderful. Come in."

Today Beth wore a skirt and matching sweater of rose-tinted cashmere. But the clothes were wrinkled and her hair was mashed flat on one side. Beth led Kimberly through a shabby kitchen into a narrow parlor that smelled of fresh paint. Kimberly saw the blanket on the seedy sofa and suddenly realized, "I woke you up."

"I've had a bit of a pain. It's fine now. Sit down, I'll just go freshen up."

But no amount of time in the bathroom could disguise the glaze to Beth's eyes, or the slow manner in which she moved around the parlor. Beth asked, "Shall I make coffee?"

"No, thank you. Maybe I should come back."

"Nonsense." Beth made a process of shutting the window and settling into a high-backed chair. "Friends are permitted to see one another at their weakest and their worst."

They were also permitted to be blunt. "You look ill."

"I have had a bad spell. That's all."

"Have you seen a doctor?"

She actually smiled at that. "Far too many, and countless times. Can we please not talk about my health anymore?"

"All right." Clearly, Beth Helms liked keeping the world at a

formal distance. Another thing they had in common. Today, however, Kimberly had a secret of her own to reveal. She forced herself to say what she had practiced the entire way over. "I find myself in a position that has never come up before. To be frank, I'm not even sure how this would be covered in the professional texts. But I think I should err on the side of caution."

Beth's only response was to fold her hands in her lap. She did not speak. It was one of the things that Kimberly admired about her. She seemed most comfortable when offering another person the gift of rapt attention. Kimberly went on, "We are friends, yes. But you and I began on a professional footing. And because of this, I feel I should tell you that I intend to date your son."

The addled sheen to Beth's gaze dissolved. "What exactly are we talking about here?"

"I . . . I don't . . ."

"Because it seems to me that a *date* is so inconsequential as to go unnoticed." Her words turned crisp, as though the discussion was precisely what she needed to draw the world back into focus. "But *feelings,* now, they are another thing entirely."

Kimberly found herself gripped by a sudden urge to confess her experience on the church front lawn. The impossible message, the impossible situation. Impossible. All of it.

"If you are simply *dating* my son, well, it's hardly a concern of mine," Beth went on. "I would not *dream* of interfering in my son's casual nightlife. He is an adult. He is free to do whatever he wills. I have no interest in discussing such issues with someone who treats my son with casual disregard." Beth's precision was smoothed by her refined diction. "On the other hand, if you actually had feelings for my boy, then I could not think of anyone I would *rather* open up to. About all *manner* of things."

"What if it didn't work out between Buddy and me?"

"Who can say what the future holds? Certainly not I. The question is, what is the situation now? How real are the feelings that have brought you to the point where you feel a need to bring this up?"

Kimberly replied slowly, "I don't think I'm ready to discuss that yet."

"Then I suggest that we leave things until you are." She closed that subject by glancing out the window and sighing. "I went to see Jack the other night. It proved to be futile. At least that is how it appears now. Even so, in those dark hours when I tend to fret, I know a remarkable sense of rightness."

Kimberly had no idea how to respond. There was a uniqueness to the situation. Being friends, and yet sensing that Beth wanted more. Whether the older woman's desires were related to herself or her son, Kimberly had no idea. So she asked, "How did you and your husband meet?"

"I first set eyes on Jack at a revival. He and I were students together at UC Davis. My family has resided in the Central Valley longer than California has been a state. My father was a dentist. He and my mother are both gone now."

"I'm so sorry."

"Thank you. But their loss has made my present situation possible. The inheritance pays my rent and expenses. Jack doesn't know about their bequest. It's the first secret I ever kept from him. I suppose I knew even then that this day was coming." She seemed to drift away for a moment, then returned with a start. "Where were we?"

"You met your husband at university."

"Actually, it was a little town, just to the east. A hamlet, really. Five churches and six taverns, and more cows than people, was how my grandfather used to describe the farming towns that anchored California's Central Valley. My grandfather was preaching at the revival, and I was there singing with our church choir.

I'll never forget the moment I saw Jack Helms. He was dressed in the finest suit, like a movie star, with his hair slicked back and his fine threads. That's how we called it. You can't imagine how dashing the man looked."

Kimberly smiled. "If he looked anything like his son does today, I can."

"If you held up a photo of Buddy today and Jack then, you'd think they were twins." Her gaze went misty. "Jack was also in pain. Granddaddy made his altar call, and Jack came forward in tears. I'd never seen a grown man cry before that day. Jack was a handsome young man carrying a whole lifetime of grief and woe. When Granddaddy asked why he had come forward, Jack screamed out the words 'I've got blood on my hands!'"

Kimberly felt her body seize up. But the woman seated across from her was too lost in memories to notice.

Beth Helms went on speaking. "Granddaddy asked Jack if he wanted to have his sins washed away. There was a lake out behind the revival tent, and they were going to have a baptismal service later that same night. But Jack wouldn't wait. Right then and there, he sort of half crawled, half ran, down to the lake. Granddaddy asked if he didn't want to change clothes and not ruin his new suit, but by that point Jack was already thigh-deep in the water. One of the women in the choir started singing the old hymn 'Nothing but the Blood,' and we all joined in, everybody just pouring out of the tent and standing there singing and watching as the pastor prayed over that handsome young man who couldn't stop crying."

Kimberly found herself taking a mental step back from the moment. It was something that often happened when she was dealing with intense issues in therapy. The space shielded her from the emotions and helped her review the situation from a professional perspective. Sometimes she wondered if it was also a crutch, a means by which she could keep herself from feeling anything too deeply.

Only that was not what happened now. Instead, she watched this woman reach into the sleeve of her sweater and draw out a tissue. She observed how Beth applied it to the corners of her eyes, though there were no tears in sight. And Kimberly had the distinct impression that everything about this moment had been carefully planned out. Including how Beth finished with the words "I do so wish Jack had held on to that power of confession and tears. Instead of wreaking vengeance on everybody who stands in his way."

CHAPTER 23

Kimberly was halfway back to her office when Buddy called. "I've got more questions than answers. But I've made a good start and I'm coming back. I need to go through what I've learned before I can be certain what to do next."

"Where are you now?"

"East of Paso Robles, about two hours from home. You mind if I use you as a sounding board?"

She hesitated only an instant. "There is nothing I would rather do than talk with you."

That stopped him. "Wow."

She nodded slowly in silent agreement. *Wow.*

Buddy described the drive and the valley and the old man's words. "It was the Keller Canneries over by Hamlin. Pop was involved."

"You think or you know?"

"I don't have a smoking gun. But the evidence is pretty strong. I've gone through the newspaper accounts from that period at the local library. The Keller family was notorious for coming down hard on the union organizers. Around the time that Pop left his hometown, there was a pair of vicious attacks. One was at a new cannery, west of Visalia, right when Pop came back driving a new car. The second was the summer before Pop entered college."

Kimberly found herself returning to the conversation with Beth. And how Buddy's mother had referred to her first meeting with Jack Helms.

"This second attack happened outside the Keller headquarters," Buddy went on. "Three striking factory workers died. The newspaper carried several reports about how a young strikebreaker was the primary suspect, but he'd vanished. They had no name. Just a description. It sounds a lot like Pop."

Kimberly pulled into the church parking lot. "I really want to hear everything. But I've got a session starting in four minutes."

"Sure. Can I call you when I get home?"

"Buddy, have dinner with me tonight."

She could almost hear the mental gears shift over the phone. The silence lasted long enough for her to become genuinely fearful he was going to turn her down. Then he said, "You mean, like a date?"

"That's right, I'm asking you on a date."

"Do you think it's a good idea?"

"Yes, Buddy. I do. I'm scheduled to meet this afternoon with a therapist in Miramar Bay. She's retiring and wants to pass over some of her patients. I can't say for certain when I'll be done."

"Let's meet there. There's a restaurant I've heard about for years. Castaways."

After she cut the connection, Kimberly sat there, thinking about what she had just done. She had gone on a few dates since the disaster of Jason, but not any since arriving in San Luis Obispo. What carried her up the stairs and into the church office was how much she wanted this to happen.

The receptionist greeted her by saying, "Your appointment just canceled. Which is good, because the pastor . . . here he comes now."

Ross Burridge strode down the hall. "Kimberly. Could you join us in my office?"

Kimberly followed the pastor out of the counseling center's rear entrance, across the lot, and into the church. They entered a wood-lined study with shelves crammed to overflowing. Ross Burridge might like his golf game and his crony status with the city's movers and shakers. But he was also a serious scholar of ancient biblical texts, which he read in the original Greek, Hebrew, and Aramaic. To her surprise, Preston was already seated in front of the pastor's desk. "What's going on?"

"Have a seat, please."

"I'll stand, thanks."

"Suit yourself." Ross fitted himself onto the window ledge. It was a position she had often seen him take, pretending at a relaxed stance while holding himself aloof from whatever tension or argument might be pervading his space. "I just got off the phone with Jack Helms. He wants the pair of you gone. Today."

Preston swiveled in his seat so as to study her. "Did he show up for counseling today?"

"Absolutely not."

Ross Burridge was handsome even when frowning. "Jack Helms is coming to you for therapy?"

"His wife made appointments, hoping the sessions would be for them both. But he has not shown up."

"How often have you seen his wife?"

"When Jack rejected her request, Beth opted not to have therapy at all." She debated whether to mention they were becoming friends, but decided now was not the time. "His daughter Carey is seeing me."

"How often?"

"Whenever there is serious emotional issues, and I have the time, I offer a new patient the chance to come in daily for the first week or so."

"And are there? Serious emotional issues, I mean."

"I'm sorry, Ross, I can't be asked to divulge anything that emerges in therapy."

"No. Of course not. Forget I ask."

"And Buddy is seeing me for therapy," Preston added. "Once so far. He's made a second appointment for tomorrow."

Ross Burridge looked genuinely alarmed. "You have two of Jack's children coming in for therapy? Why wasn't I informed?"

Preston countered, "Why should we have told you anything at all?"

"The most difficult elder this church has ever known? I realize you two have just arrived. But surely you must have noticed what an effect Jack has."

Preston held his ground. "Even so, my question still stands."

"That should be clear enough. Part of every pastor's job is political. The worst part, as far as I'm concerned. Jack Helms personally arranged for my predecessor's dismissal. I've managed to avoid his wrath for nine years. I want to keep it that way."

Kimberly decided he needed to hear the rest. "It gets worse, I'm afraid. Beth Helms has left her husband."

Ross looked aghast. "You can't be serious."

"She has taken an apartment in old town."

"All right. I've heard enough. Thank you for your time."

Preston waited until he was at the door to ask, "What about us? Do we pack?"

But the pastor's only response was to run a hand through his groomed silver hair and mutter, "What a mess."

CHAPTER 24

Once she arrived home, Kimberly did not allow the day's conversations and crises and conflicts to crowd in. If she had, she would have called the whole thing off. And she didn't want that. For the first time in four long years, she was excited about spending time with a man.

The suitcase was in the back of her closet, where she had put it upon moving in. It had occupied a similar position in Seattle since the week after her divorce became final. Packing the case had been her way of coming to terms with the fact that her life was going to be lonely from then on. She had trained herself not to look at the case, or remember what the contents once had meant. Kimberly set the suitcase on the bed, then found herself unable to open the latches.

She poured herself a bath and added her favorite eucalyptus-scented wash. She shaved her legs and plucked her eyebrows. She took forever on her makeup. She brushed and brushed her hair, then fashioned a French twist. Then she returned to the bedroom. The case was there, waiting for her. Beckoning. Threatening her with the pain of hope.

She forced herself to open the latches. The dresses were still in the plastic wrapping from their last dry cleaning. Eight outfits, with a small jewelry box on top. Four pairs of shoes lined the sides. It would have been too much to ask for the memories and the regret to leave her untouched. But at least the bitter agony was gone.

She had bought the top outfit to wear for her last formal event with Jason. The corporate gathering had taken place the night before she told him she was carrying his child. Jason had claimed to like showing her off. He had always said he was proud of her beauty. He had liked to go shopping with her for these items, sitting in the room while she modeled one outfit after another.

The dress was by Versace, a midnight-blue silk so dark it appeared black in certain lights. It was designed like an Art Deco cheongsam, high-shouldered and clinging to her like a second skin. One row of the silk buttons traced straight up and down, while the other curved around to meet her right shoulder. The dress on that side was slit in the Oriental fashion, only a little, for the skirt was already quite short. Kimberly buttoned herself into the frock, then slipped her hands over her hips, straightening the lines and pulling out four years of wrinkles. She put on the matching diamond-patterned tights, then slipped on the Ferragamo pumps, with the impossible heels and the little gold straps. She debated whether to add the pearls, alternating white and smoky gray, then decided not. She closed her case and turned for the first time to meet her reflection in the mirror. Kimberly could not help but smile at the thought that Buddy would probably not mind a few wrinkles.

When she came downstairs, Preston took one look and said, "Call out the dogs."

She held out the hand not holding the small alligator purse. "You like?"

"Just tell me what you did with my cousin and I'll let you go."

She kissed the air by his cheek, determined not to smudge

her lipstick. "She's still here on the inside. Trying hard to pretend everything will be okay."

Preston gave her the signature look, the one that filled her with the memory of the second father, who was now lost to them both. Straight to the heart. "You are doing great, and you are getting even better."

When Buddy had suggested they meet at Castaways, he had only told Kimberly half the truth. Miramar Bay possessed a sort of locals-only legend. It was said that it held the power to offer second chances—at life, at love, whatever the individual most held dear. After the break-up with Shona, Buddy had started driving up almost every weekend, walking the coastal path and hoping against hope that breathing the salt tang might help reshape his future.

Now he arrived early enough to park in the beachside lot and join the others out to enjoy a sunset stroll. His nice clothes garnered a few looks, but not many. Even well-dressed folks could find themselves in need of another chance. The question, he now knew, was not being offered a new opportunity; it was avoiding the mistakes he had made the first time around.

He entered Castaways ten minutes before they were scheduled to meet. The restaurant's western wall held the largest bay window he had ever seen, with panes so old the glass had run, turning dusk's final glimmers into rainbows on the old wooden paneling.

When the young woman entered the restaurant, Buddy had no idea who she was. What he noticed most was the way everyone stared. Not just the men. Everyone in the place watched her. Then he was struck by the double-barreled shock. First, that it was Kimberly. Second, that the hostess was bringing this gorgeous woman to *his table*.

The way she walked, precisely placing each foot down directly in front of the other, left him suspecting she had not been in heels for a long time. She passed the bar and crossed the restaurant to where he stood, ignoring the attention that followed her. Up close the view even got better, the overlarge eyes and the glistening lips. She must have noticed his nerves, though, for she allowed the restaurant host to seat her, waited for Buddy to settle back into his own chair, then leaned across and asked, "What's the matter?"

"You look fabulous."

"Thank you, Buddy. Now tell me what's wrong."

He waved away the waiter. "I should have worn a suit."

"You'll have to do better than that."

"Kimberly, you are the most beautiful . . ." He lowered his gaze to his hands. Forced his brain to punch through the shock, and come face-to-face with what had frightened him so. "I haven't been on a date in almost three years. Since my girlfriend told me she couldn't trust me. I didn't understand what she was talking about. I hadn't done anything, never cheated, hardly even looked at another woman. But she wouldn't listen. She left me."

Kimberly whispered, "She broke your heart."

"I'd never loved anyone before. I didn't think anyone could hurt me like that. Nobody except . . ."

"No one, save your father."

"The day after I moved Mom into her new place, she told me something . . . I went to see Shona. It was the first time we'd spoken since the week after she broke things off." He took a hard breath. "I asked her the real reason why she had dumped me. She said she didn't know who I was. And she thought I didn't, either. And she was right."

"Buddy, I want you to look at me." When he didn't move, she reached across the table and gripped his chin and lifted his gaze to her own. "Tell me what you're feeling right now."

His tremors were so tight, the words were fractured. "I'm so scared."

"I understand. I really do. The last time I wore this dress was four years ago. I was thrilled and excited because the next day I was going to tell my ex that I was carrying his child. I felt giddy with excitement and joy. I had never felt so alive. I spent all that night thinking how happy I was, that I couldn't wait to share this incredible news. First with Jason, then Preston and his parents and all these other people who were lined up in my head, the people I cared most for in the world. Only I never did make those calls. Because the next day Jason told me he didn't want the child. And he didn't want me."

Buddy opened his mouth, but the words weren't there. He could drown in her perfume. In the glistening depths of her gaze. In the soft lament.

She went on. "So I folded up the dress and I packed it away. And it's been there ever since. I'm telling you this because I want you to know that I am scared, too."

"I guess that should make me feel better. But it doesn't."

"I didn't tell you this because I wanted to comfort you. I wanted to share with you. I haven't shared this with anyone outside my family."

"What do I do now?"

"You can take my hand if you like."

He felt as though he was crossing entire continents, reaching across the table. Her hand was exactly as he would have expected. Long fingers, supple strength, a slight shadow of an indentation where a ring once lay. "I'm so sorry, Kimberly."

"I didn't tell you for sympathy."

"I know." He liked the feel of her hand so much he reached across with his other. "What happens now?"

"We're on a date, Buddy. Accept it and let's move on."

"I'll try." And he would. For her.

CHAPTER 25

Hours later, Buddy did not so much drive home as drift back on a perfumed cloud. He was glad to find Carey already in bed, as he needed a bit more time before trying to talk about this with anyone, even his sister.

He was easing into his pallet when his cell phone rang. He had forgotten to cut it off, which only highlighted how far the evening with Kimberly had swept him away. He checked the readout, did not recognize the number, and decided he had no interest in talking with anyone other than Kimberly. He let it ring.

Then it went quiet, only for the house phone to start. He hurried into the kitchen. "Hello?"

Kimberly's voice sounded very different from before. "I know it's late, but this couldn't wait until morning. Is your sister awake?"

"She's right here." Buddy turned to his sleep-tousled sister standing by the bedroom door. "It's Kimberly."

"While we were away, Preston took a call from Ross Burridge, the senior pastor. There's to be a gathering of church elders tomorrow morning. They intend to dismiss us both."

His former bliss disappeared like smoke in a hurricane. "Pop is behind this."

"Apparently so." She sighed. "Your father came to see me."

"When?"

"Monday. He threatened to have me fired if I counseled your mother. I'm sorry, Buddy, I probably should have said something before now. But then Beth decided she didn't want therapy, in any case, and you and I, well . . ."

"I understand."

Carey demanded, "What's going on?"

"Pop is going after Kimberly and Preston. Because of us." Buddy lifted his hand to stop her response before it was formed. *Wait.* He said into the phone, "What can we do?"

"I have no idea. Probably not a lot. I just wanted you to know."

"When is it happening?"

"Eleven-thirty. Which means I need to cancel the session with Carey."

"I'll tell sis."

"I was going to call her next."

"She's right here. Let me do it. We need to talk this through."

"Ross met us this morning. He said your father has been on the rampage. Again, in retrospect I should have told you. But I didn't want to have this taint our time together."

"I'm glad you didn't." He leaned his forehead against the wall. "Kimberly, I'm so sorry."

"I am also. You're a good man. This should not be happening to you."

"I meant—"

"I know what you meant. And thank you."

Buddy hung up the phone and immediately started dialing. He told his sister, "Mom needs to hear this, too."

His mother took the news in silence, then said, "We can't let this happen."

Buddy saw the stricken look on his sister's face, and felt the old helpless burn. "It already has."

"Not this time. Not to these good people, who have done nothing but be there for us when we needed help most." Beth Helms used the same voice she adopted when scolding one of them. "That poor deluded man. I could wring his neck."

"I'll make some—"

"No, Buddy. You're going to leave this to me."

"Mom, I know a lot of the people involved in setting up the clinic. I could—"

"The elders involved are *my* friends." Despite her ire, Beth's voice sounded slightly blurred. "Most I've known longer than you have been alive. For once, you are *not* going to take charge."

Buddy felt himself smile, which given the hour and the circumstances he took as a good sign. "All right, Mom."

"How was your date?"

"Let's leave that for another time."

"Get some rest, Buddy. Carey too. Tomorrow will be a long day."

"What about you?"

"I've been asleep long enough."

CHAPTER 26

But despite her best intentions, Beth only managed two phone calls. She had taken a second pain medication just before Buddy delivered the news. She was forced to stop when the fog rolled in. To continue would have meant confessing her own issues. Her children needed to hear that first. And soon.

The next morning she drank an entire pot of coffee and completed her calls before eight, waking two of her friends and catching two others as they were shepherding children off to school. Then she made the most important call of all, pressing for an appointment with an extremely busy man, using all the honeyed guile she could muster. It left her weary, and the day would be a long one. So she knocked on her neighbor's door, and confessed, "I can't do what today requires without your help."

Josiah drove her to the Sierra Vista Medical Center in an Oldsmobile of considerable vintage. The car was immaculate, though the mileage was near stratospheric. Beth knew because she leaned over to check. Josiah smiled and said, "This sweet lady will outlive us both."

"No argument there." She liked how he drove, applying the caution of a man comfortable with his own limits. "Thank you for doing this."

"It's part of being a good neighbor."

She studied Josiah, taking in the innate strength and dignity. "And friends."

"I'd certainly like to think so." He took a corner like a vessel under sail. "Your son has the makings of a great man."

There was no reason for the words to press tears from her eyes. "Yes. He does."

They did not speak again until he pulled into the parking lot, and Josiah asked, "Does Buddy know about your condition?"

"No. None of the children do."

"Are you wise to wait?"

"I felt I had to." She liked the way the morning carved his features into a honeyed icon. "They've had so much on their plates. I didn't want to add more."

"I understand that. But time has a way of making party hats out of our best intentions."

"I'll tell them as soon as this issue has been resolved. This one thing."

He watched her fumble for the door. "You need my help?"

"No, thank you. I can manage."

"Take your time, Beth. I'll be right here when you're done."

She thanked him and entered the doctor's office building adjacent to the acute medical center. There was a definite gradation to Beth's day. The pain was always there. She suspected it had become a permanent component to her days. She could feel the foreign substance invading her body, etching itself into her life. She knew her time was ending. All these things were facts. She had no interest in fighting them—even if it was possible, which it wasn't. And yet she was determined not to make that the center of her existence.

She sat in the doctor's office, surrounded by people who were deeply angry over their fate. She saw the bitter unfairness etched into their faces, the resigned sorrow, the fear. Whether or not they survived, they faced months of uncertainty and pain, perhaps years. Their lives would never be the same. They were hurting and isolated. They wanted nothing more than to be somewhere else. Then there were the others. Two ladies and one young man who all wore scarves over their bald heads, who sat with eyes shut, who listened to music over their iPods. Those three expressions held a parallel serenity. Beth understood them. They were intent upon defying the others and their bitter act of surrender. They managed to eke out a fragment of peace, of goodness. Even here. Just like Beth. The young man opened his eyes then, as though he could feel the intensity of Beth's scrutiny. He smiled at her. Sharing their secret insolence.

"Mrs. Helms? How are you today? Won't you come this way?"

The nurse led Beth into the back office, timing her steps to match her own. The doctor she worked for, Clayton Sharpe, was not a pleasant man. The first few times they had met, Beth had been taken aback by his brusqueness. The man carried himself with a barely suppressed impatience, a secret fury. Now she understood. Clayton was a brawler by nature. He had dedicated his life to doing battle, most of which he would not win. The oncologist kept making notes in a file as she seated herself across from his desk. "Have you told your family yet?"

"Some of them. Yes."

"You can't put this off any longer, Beth."

"That's not why I'm here today."

"But it's an issue that you have to face." He slapped the file shut and glared at her. Clayton Sharpe was probably in his mid-forties, but his gaze had been turned ancient by having stared into too many graves. "How is the pain?"

"Getting worse."

"Do you need something stronger?"

"No, thank you."

"You will. Soon enough. Just like you'll need to think about hospice care." He opened her file, scanned the top sheet, and said, "You've moved to an apartment in Old Town?"

"I have taken a small apartment. It suits me."

"By yourself? That won't do. Not for much longer." He shot her another hard look. "Avoiding the discussion with your family will not put off the inevitable by one single day."

"I told you, that's not why I'm here. I want you to do something for me. You're an elder in our church. It's one of the reasons I chose you as my doctor."

As she explained what she wanted, the doctor's impatience gradually eased. He sensed a battle. And a cause.

"Your husband," he declared, "is a bully."

"He wasn't always. But now . . . I could not agree more."

He tapped his pen on the open file. "When is the meeting?"

"In three hours."

"If I do this, will you agree to tell your family?"

"Of course. Yes." She sighed around a sudden stab, as though releasing her tension allowed the pain more room to expand. "I'll go tell my daughter right now."

CHAPTER 27

The pain crimped Beth's side such that Josiah was up and moving before she had fully emerged from the doctor's building. He took their return journey at her pace, eased her into the car, then settled behind the wheel. He tapped the gearshift a few times, then said, "You got every reason in the world to tell me it ain't none of my business."

"I know. I need to tell my family."

"That's right. You surely do."

"Could you drive me to my son's home?"

"You mean, right now?"

The simple act of deciding had heightened her discomfort. As though the admission finally gave the pain a freer rein. "Yes. While I still can."

He started the car. "Will he even be there?"

"No. Which is why we need to go now."

He turned from the parking lot. "You do realize you're not making any sense."

It was the last thing Josiah said. She spoke only to give him directions. When he parked in front of Buddy's town house, Josiah cut the motor and walked around to her door and helped her up. She did not let go of his arm, which was all he required to walk her to the front door. When she rang the bell, he settled her hand on the side rail and said, "I'll be waiting in the car."

"Josiah." When he turned back, she went on, "You are one of God's secret angels."

His reply was cut off by Carey opening the door. "Momma, what are you doing here?"

"But, Momma, you *can't* just *die.*"

Beth sat and held Carey's hand and let her daughter weep. Somewhere outside a dog barked. Through the living-room window she could see the nose of Josiah's car. She had always disliked relying on other people for help. In the past such moments had usually left her wondering if people aided her out of sympathy for the woman who put up with Jack Helms. She didn't want their pity. But she was going to have to grow accustomed to accepting help. "All right. That's enough."

"How long have you known?"

"You've asked me that already."

"Why didn't you tell me before now?"

"Because you had your own troubles. Dry your eyes. We need to talk."

Carey sniffed loudly. "What are we doing now?"

"We're letting you get used to some unwanted news. I'm sorry I had to break it like this. I always thought I'd be telling Buddy first, and then we'd come to you together."

Her brisk attitude dampened Carey's ability to gush tears. "I don't understand."

"Buddy has spent his entire life being strong for you. Now is your chance to do something for him."

"Momma . . . we're talking about you."

"No, child. We're done with that. I'm sick and it's going to get worse. You need to accept it and move on." When Carey started to protest, Beth gripped her hand as tightly as she could and said, "Daughter, you need to *focus.*"

"You're hurting me."

Beth did not let up. There in her daughter's face was the little child who never received the love and approval she so desperately sought from her daddy. So she had gone looking for it in all the wrong places. One more in a long list of issues Beth was powerless to change. "Buddy needs you, Carey."

As she explained what she wanted, Beth saw a faint light grow in her daughter's shattered gaze. Something Beth had longed to see for years. The tiniest hint of something new. A slight glimmer of independence.

When she finished, Beth waited, willing her daughter to fight against twenty-seven years of caving in. She watched Carey wipe both cheeks with her free hand. Scarcely able to breathe.

"Daddy scares me."

"Your father can be a scary man."

She smiled then. "You've never said that before."

Beth released as much of a breath as she could manage. "I know that. And I'm sorry. I wish I had done a better job . . . but never mind that. We simply don't have time for regrets."

"When do you think we'll need to do this?"

"I have no idea. Soon. Jack has no patience when it comes to a fight. And from what Buddy tells me, the situation they face in the company is a time bomb."

When Carey shivered, Beth could only hope there was a hint of excitement mixed with the very real fear. "I can't believe we're having this conversation."

"Daughter, look at me. Two very important things. First, you mustn't tell Buddy about my condition. I'm phoning your sister as soon as I arrive home. If you need to talk to someone, do so with her. But you must let me tell Buddy in my own time."

"But—"

"No arguments. Please. I don't have the strength." She waited until she was certain Carey understood, then continued. "And second, knowing Jack as I do, we must assume that we won't have much warning. You need to be ready to move very swiftly when the time comes."

"I'll do it. For Buddy." She shivered, but she also smiled, the tiny wounded child alight in her eyes. "And for you."

"Thank you, darling." Beth reached out to hug her baby girl. "I knew I could rely on you."

CHAPTER 28

At the meeting of the elders, Kimberly and Preston were asked to wait in the church council's antechamber. The senior pastor gathered with a number of the church's deacons and elders in the main conference room. Kimberly had some vague idea of what was going to happen, a formal question-and-answer session. She had done nothing wrong. She was as prepared as she could be. She had her cousin for company. The last time she had confronted a group of examiners, she had been sitting for her counseling degree. She had not slept the night before that, either.

Then Buddy entered the waiting room, and offered them both a tentative smile. She rose to greet him, then accepted hugs from Beth Helms and Carey, both of whom carried their own evident strain. "Thank you all for coming."

"What nonsense, thanking us for something that our family has caused." Beth hugged her again. It was the first time they had ever touched, and it left Kimberly's eyes burning. "How are you, dear?"

"Coping."

The senior pastor's door opened. Ross Burridge shook Buddy's hand, greeted Beth and Carey, and announced, "It appears that your father is not coming."

"He wouldn't," Buddy agreed. "Not unless he was certain of victory."

"He has sent his lawyer," Ross said.

"The gall of that man is astonishing, even to me," Beth said.

Ross started to object, then thought better of it. "Well, I suppose we had best get started."

The allies of Jack Helms among the church elders sought to distance themselves by directing Kimberly and Preston to the long conference table's far end. But their isolation was erased when Beth Helms insisted upon sitting next to Kimberly, and Carey stood with Buddy against the back wall.

The church leaders were seated around the table's opposite end, with a few latecomers standing behind them. The women were mostly gray-heads with appearances as shellacked and polished as their opinions. The men were well-fleshed and most wore dark suits. Kimberly was tempted to simply get up and walk away. She didn't need this. She hated confrontation and always had. But to leave meant letting Jack Helms win. Some things were worth fighting for.

Ross Burridge opened the conversation. "For the record we're gathered to discuss a matter tabled by Jack Helms. He has not joined us, though he called this meeting."

Jack's attorney, a pasty-faced man by the name of Grady White, cleared his throat. "Mr. Helms asked me to express his sincere regrets. But he has been called away at the last minute. Urgent business matters."

"Noted." Ross Burridge wore his CEO face, somber and commanding. "So that we are all clear, Preston, why don't you two give us a brief overview of your role and duties within the church."

"We've been through all that," a man by the back wall protested. "Before they were hired."

"Some of us were not present for those discussions, Dr. Sharpe," Ross pointed out.

"The church voted as a whole." He was dressed in what Kimberly considered medical casual. Very expensive clothes, with a matching attitude that suggested he was used to having the hospital staff jump at his command. "We all agreed these two in-house therapists were needed. I don't see why we're meeting at all."

"Nonetheless we are here." Ross motioned to Preston. "Please."

She and Preston had agreed he would speak for them. Preston was seminary trained and had been at the church several months longer. Plus, he was better at keeping his temper. Even so, Kimberly knew he was riled at the outset. "You ran an advertisement for professional counselors who also had pastoral training. I applied. You hired me. I don't see what else needs to be said."

"Just the same, let's go into a bit more detail for the sake of those gathered here," Ross replied. "Describe for us your role, as you see it."

"My job description is clearly set out in the contract you wrote. I am to give first position to all patients who are members of these four local congregations. Those who can pay will be charged the hourly fee, which you set. But my services will not be restricted by ability to pay. Beyond these patients, I am free to take others from the wider community. My contract also lays out this fee schedule, a third of which goes back to the clinic."

One of the gray-haired women at the table demanded, "And what is *she* doing here?"

"Kimberly was hired to take over the position of your school counselor, who is retiring in May," Preston replied. "You moved up her start date because she was available, and because there was an unexpectedly high demand for counseling services."

The man by the back wall demanded, "What does that mean, 'unexpectedly high demand'?"

"I am already overbooked."

Dr. Sharpe had an aggressive attitude and very little patience. "So you hired them. They know their role. The demand for their services is high. I ask again, why are we here?"

The gray-haired matron turned to Ross. "How much is this costing us?"

"Nothing," Ross replied flatly. "They are taking in considerably more than their combined salaries."

"For the third time," the man by the back wall said, "what are we doing here?"

The gray-haired lady snapped, "There's been a complaint."

"By a man who is not a patient," Preston replied. "And who could not be bothered to show up."

"Now see here," Grady protested, "I won't stand for such talk."

"Why not?" Preston shot back. "You expect us to sit here and lap up whatever nonsense you throw our way?"

The woman bridled. "This is *not* nonsense."

"It's ridiculous," Preston replied. "If you won't back us in such a situation, why were we taken on in the first place?"

The man by the back wall said, "That is *exactly* the question I'd like to hear answered."

Buddy chose that moment to speak. "You're asking the wrong person."

Grady White pointed an indignant finger at Buddy. "That man has no right addressing these proceedings."

"You are not the one to decide that," Ross replied. "I am."

Buddy went on, "The reason we're here is because I've resigned from my father's company and as a result he stands to lose his single greatest contract—"

"I protest!" Grady's annoyance was genuine now. "This meeting is about those two fakirs on your payroll."

Kimberly could not help it. She laughed out loud. "What century are you living in?"

"You know my father," Buddy raised his voice. "You know his favorite tactic is attack. He despises anyone who sees the world through a different lens than his own. He views Kimberly and Preston as a threat."

The oldest lady declared, "The whole concept of church-sponsored therapy is vile." Two of the others seated around the table nodded.

A gentleman seated at the far end glanced nervously at Beth, cleared his throat, and said, "With respect I disagree."

Ross inspected the opponents. "Why didn't any of you raise your objections before now?"

"The church wanted them. I knew it was a mistake. We all did. But these young people . . . It's creeping liberalism, that's what it is."

The effort Preston needed to keep a lid on his anger showed in bright spots on his cheeks. "Do you feel the same way about medical treatment?"

"Of course not. They're hardly the same."

"So let me get this straight. You consider any form of counseling, be it for grief or loss or past wounds, to be something akin to witchcraft?"

She reddened. "I am not the one on trial here, you are!"

"There's no trial," Ross corrected.

"I want them *out* of here!"

"Well, I don't," the man by the back wall replied. "I want to hear what is going on inside Jack Helms's family."

Grady protested, "How can you besmirch my client's good name when he's not here to defend himself?"

The man would not back down. "Because he called this meeting. And I, for one, want *answers.*"

Beth sat up straighter. "Might I have a word?"

"Go ahead, Beth," Ross said.

Beth said, "I left my husband this week."

One of the elders moaned, "Oh, Beth."

"I hope and pray this separation is temporary. I took this step because Jack needs to change course. I have spent years being the peacemaker, a task I actually enjoyed in some respects. But it has allowed Jack to move farther down a road that I want him to turn away from." Beth paused and took a long breath. She then spoke to her hands folded upon the table. "I love my husband dearly. Despite all his faults. And foremost among them is, Jack Helms has become a bully."

When Grady started to object, Ross halted him with a warning finger. "You will let her speak and you will not interrupt."

"Jack has forced all of his children to leave him. Sylvie is in Vancouver and hasn't been home in eight years," Beth went on. "Carey, well, I'll let her speak for herself if she wants."

"I don't," Carey said. "Except to say that it's true."

"Buddy is the last to leave. He clung on longer than I thought possible, given the way Jack has treated him. But he left, and as he said, his departure threatens the company's future."

"That is *not* true," Grady protested.

"Quiet, you. Go on, Beth."

"No, wait a moment, please." The man by the back wall stepped to where he dominated that side of the table. "I'm still not clear on why Jack went after the church's new therapists."

"Because we have entered counseling," Beth replied.

"What, *all* of you?"

"That is correct. Carey and I are seeing Kimberly. Buddy is meeting with Preston. It is something I would rather not discuss, but the simple fact is, we are all carrying our burdens from life with Jack Helms, and we need help. And these two fine people are giving us what we need. And Jack is going after them for the simple reason that he can. Because you are allowing it."

The woman protested, "I, for one, am most *certainly* not here because of Jack!"

"No. And you have every right to disapprove. But you

would not be going against a majority of the church member-ship if it were not for my husband. And if you let him win here today, two innocent people, who are already a vital component of this community, will suffer. Undeservedly so."

Ross called for a vote, and by a slim majority the two of them kept their jobs. Preston clearly found no satisfaction in the result. He was the first to depart, trailing smoke and cinders behind him. Kimberly held back because she intended to thank Buddy and his mother. Which meant she was there to see Buddy walk over to Grady and say, "I want you to pass on something to my father."

Grady blustered, "My duties hardly include playing messenger boy. Tell him yourself."

"Jack's gone too far this time. It's one thing for him to attack me. He's been doing it for years. But this time he's stepped over the boundary. He's trying to harm two people who made the mistake of doing the right thing by me and my family. He won't get away with it."

The two men were locked in a generational struggle, which meant they missed how the entire room held its breath. Even the conservative guard remained seated at the table's other end. They all realized something major was taking place.

Beth said softly, "Buddy . . ."

"Tell my father he is going to get the fight he's asking for," Buddy went on. He lowered his face, down to where the menace caused the attorney to cringe away. "And he's going to get the results he deserves."

CHAPTER 29

Buddy paced back and forth across Preston's office because he had to. He was filled with jagged emotions that shredded each breath and kept him from sitting down. He knew he was aping his father's actions, and knew also there was nothing he could do about it. Preston sat behind his desk, waiting. Buddy said, "I'm so sorry this happened."

"So am I." A residual from the morning's emotions still grated in Preston's voice. "But we're not here to talk about that. We're here to discuss you and your situation. So apology accepted. Now let's move on."

But the problem was, Buddy couldn't. It was one thing to step away from his father's grip. It was another thing entirely to defy him. The trail of Buddy's years was littered with the corpses of people who had thought they could go up against Jack Helms. But it was more than simple fear. "It has to be done."

"What does?"

Buddy did not respond. The words that emerged were only the trailing edge of the argument raging within.

"Buddy. Look at me."

He glanced over on his next circuit of the carpet.

"Tell me what you're thinking."

"I need to stop him."

"Jack Helms. Your father."

"That's right. Soon as I figure out how."

"Why is that, Buddy? Why do you need to defeat your father?"

"You know why. You just saw why. He's a menace."

"A menace to whom?"

Buddy saw a hint of something behind the questions. He had no idea what it was. Even so, the hidden meaning resonated enough to slow him down.

"Who is it that is threatened, Buddy?"

"Me, for certain."

"But he's threatened you for years. Why are you going after him now?"

Buddy looked over a second time. "He didn't just threaten. He *attacked* me."

"That's right, he did." The act of counseling returned Preston to an alert calm. "But what else is different this time?"

Buddy decided he had to sit down for whatever came next.

"He attacked people you care about. Isn't that right?"

"Yes."

"He has come after your *team*. Remember what we said about that last time? Who is your team, Buddy?"

He opened his mouth, shut it, and finally came up with, "People I care about."

"Who else?"

There was no reason why the realization should emerge like a confession. "People who trust me."

Preston smiled. Back in his element now. The piercing clarity of a man doing what he was born and trained to do. Finding wisdom in the storm of life. "People who bind themselves to you by choice. Isn't that right?"

No reason why it should leave him raw. No reason at all. "Yes."

"The last time we met, I said I thought you should hear some truths that normally require a great deal of time to emerge. I'm going to continue in that same vein. This admission of yours is important for two reasons. First, because very often in situations where young people face trauma, they carry with them a burden of guilt. As though they somehow deserved their fate." Preston leaned his elbows on the table. "So I want you to ask yourself, how many people in Jack Helms's orbit are there because they trust him, because they *want* to place their lives in his hands?"

"None. Zip."

"Precisely. I want you to think on that between now and the next time we meet. Will you do that?"

"All right, yes."

"Fine." Preston leaned back and swiveled his chair around. Aiming his words at the sidewall. Freeing Buddy from the force of his gaze. "So let's move on. What do you think this has to say about your five-year goals?"

"I don't . . ."

"You feel so tied to people that share with you the gift of trust that you are going against a lifetime's habit of avoiding conflict with your father. So this is important to you. Vital, even. How can you state this in terms of your goals, of where you want to be in five years?"

The answer was there before Preston completed his sentence. He extracted the creased paper from his pocket. When he looked up, Preston still examined some point on his sidewall. Giving him space. Letting him define the moment. "I want to deserve their trust."

"But aren't you already doing that? Don't they follow you

now, even when it is dangerous for them to do so?" Preston glanced over. "Go back to the original question. Who is your team?"

"I don't . . . You're saying I need to *expand* my team."

"Is that what you want?"

Buddy did not reply.

"Right now, you're limiting your team to people who trust *you*. Who come to *you*. What about people you need to trust? Are they included in your team?"

It was his turn to nod slowly. "I have trouble with that. Trusting people."

"So now we're talking about another five-year goal, wouldn't you say?"

His mind returned to the beautiful eyes that had captured him the night before. He could not remember exactly what Kimberly had said. But he could hear her voice. A hymn of hope and days yet undefined.

Buddy bent over his page and wrote not one new goal, but two. The first, however, was the only one he said aloud. "To learn to trust, and to learn to identify those I should trust."

"And be willing to make mistakes in the meantime," Preston said, just as the clock chimed. "Time's up for today."

Buddy thanked him and left. He stood in the hall and took his time refolding the page, giving himself a long moment to embed the second goal on his heart. What he had written down was, *To break free of these chains, and to love, really love, without pain or the past making the rules.*

Then he put the page in his pocket, stowing everything about those thoughts down deep. Because as soon as he left this church, this haven, he was going on the attack. Against the most dangerous man in his universe. His father. And the problem was, he had no idea how he was going to do that. None at all.

Kimberly decided to cancel the day's remaining sessions. The receptionist accepted the news with the aplomb of a woman who had endured her own share of church dramas. She printed out Kimberly's appointments and together they started calling.

Kimberly passed Preston's office just as her cousin was shutting his door. She caught a glimpse of Buddy pacing the floor, and felt her insides wrenched by his tension. She saw the morning's impact etched upon the taut features of a man she would like to claim as her own. She entered her office, shut the door, seated herself behind the desk, and took a long breath. She knew precisely what she was going to do. She had made her decision before leaving the conference room. She did not hesitate through indecision. She just needed a moment to accept the deeper significance behind her resolve.

She heard muted male voices from the room next door, and knew what it signified. She had witnessed Buddy deliver the message to the pale, chubby lawyer. Buddy was going after his father.

But she had also witnessed the aftermath of Jack Helms's vengeance. It was there in the bruised souls of all his family. She worried how Buddy, strong as he might be, could ever find a way to win.

She had known before the elders voted that she was going to help him. Whether or not the church kept them on, Kimberly was on his side. She was frightened by what this sort of commitment meant, but she was also determined.

She cleared away her files and took out a pad and pen. The question she needed to answer was simple enough. What could she bring to the table that Buddy would not have on his own? Support, of course. She would offer that, and she would be there to put what salve she could on his wounds. The thought that Jack Helms might further abrade her man's spirit left her quaking with anger. It was a potent force. As Jack Helms was about to find out.

Buddy had given her a detailed explanation of his trip to his father's hometown. Kimberly began making notes, breaking down the information as she would the components of early therapy sessions. It was the method she had developed for delving below the surface with new patients, going beyond what they said to the core issue, the motive that shaped their behavior, the hidden agenda of their unconscious mind.

As she worked, one issue rose repeatedly to the forefront. Jack Helms had left his hometown at age sixteen. Which meant he had probably not graduated from high school. From what Buddy had told her about Jack's past, he did not sound like someone who had skipped grades and graduated early. If so, how had he then enrolled in one of California's universities? It was a minor point, easily overlooked. But such fault lines often opened into portals through which the patient's hidden secrets were revealed. Buddy had mentioned his father had spent time in Hamlin. But for how long, he had no idea. Nor did he have any way to find out. The local Hamlin papers made no mention of Jack Helms. Which was hardly a surprise.

But Kimberly had avenues open to her that were barred to most people. And she was going to use them all.

She spent another quarter hour making careful notes and researching items on her laptop. Then she placed a call to the regional mental-health coordinator in Hamlin. "This is Kimberly Sturgiss, I'm a therapist based in San Luis Obispo. Is this Dr. Winters?"

"It is indeed, Dr. Sturgiss. How you doing this morning?"

"I'm fine, sir, but I'm not a doctor. I have a master's in counseling from Seattle University."

"I know the program, and you're no doubt more qualified than most doctors I deal with." He had the soothing voice of a man who applied his country manners as a healing ungent. "What can I do for you?"

"I have two patients who are the wife and daughter of a man

who spent some time in your town. There are issues related to their sessions that I can't divulge."

"No need."

"I'm calling to ask if you could help track down something."

"If I can."

"The man in question worked briefly in your city as a young man. He then studied at UC Davis. I'm trying to determine what exactly happened while he was in Hamlin. Beginning with how he attended university, even though he does not seem to have graduated from high school. At least, not in his home town."

"So you need to find out if he enrolled in school here."

"Can he, if he wasn't from there and had no family?"

"This is a small town, Miss Sturgiss. We can usually find a way to grease the wheels if there's a strong enough need. What brought this fellow down our way?"

"He was employed by a regional cannery."

"Well, we surely have our share of them."

"Could they have sponsored him? Or helped him gain a GED?"

"Absolutely. You'll need to speak to our county superintendent. Doris Hicks is her name. Let me make a call."

"I would appreciate that so much, Dr. Winters. But before you go, there is one other matter."

"Fire away."

"Can you speak with the local police and see if the man in question was ever arrested? He was not convicted, I can tell you that much. And I'm also certain his arrest records would have been sealed by the court."

"He was a minor?"

"That is what I have been led to understand. And there's something else. If he was arrested, I suspect the same friends who helped usher him through school protected him from prosecution."

"Sounds like a tough man to go after, Miss Sturgiss."

"Sir, as I said, I am simply trying to do my job as a therapist."

Winters hummed an unconvinced note. "What's the fellow's name?"

"Helms. Jack Helms."

CHAPTER 30

The midday sky was hazed a red-gold as Buddy entered the commercial zone near UCSB. He parked across the street from the Hazzard headquarters. The day held its breath, as though the city of Santa Barbara was aghast at Buddy's audacity. A vapor of apprehension slipped back and forth over the sun as Buddy crossed the street. Midday had come and gone and he had not eaten. He was too nervous to feel hunger, though he did feel hollow. His every step seemed foreordained, as though he had been focused upon this event all along. The Lexington contract and his father's response and his own departure were merely steps upon the way. He would go up against the battlements his father had spent nine years raising and arming. And he ran a real risk of being crushed as a result.

As he had requested, the Hazzard group's chief attorney was seated in Cliff's outer office, waiting for him. Stanton Parrish was every inch the silver fox, urbane where his group chairman was bluff, smooth where Cliff Hazzard wielded the hammer. The attorney shook Buddy's hand and said, "I do hope you haven't called me here for nothing."

"I have never liked anyone wasting my time," Buddy replied. "I try to apply that to every meeting I make."

"Good lad." He motioned Buddy into a seat. "Coffee?"

"Black."

"Cliff is held up with a group visiting from Tokyo. He will be with us shortly."

"I needed to speak with you as much as Cliff," Buddy replied. "Maybe more."

"I'm all ears."

Buddy handed over the court documents. Stanton drew out a pair of gold-plated reading glasses and read swiftly. "Oh, my."

"I want you to represent me."

"I see."

"I don't have any money."

"Well. That is a problem. And no doubt your father is aware of it."

"He is counting on me being helpless in the face of his attack."

"I assume you have a way around this?"

"Only if you will agree to represent me."

The attorney gave him a refined smile. "Only if I can be assured of payment."

"That's where Cliff comes in." Buddy outlined what he had in mind.

Five minutes later, the CEO marched in. "How you doing, Buddy?"

"The young man has been scalded, but has managed to survive," Stanton replied for him. "And come up with quite a remarkable approach to the crisis."

Cliff led them into his office and dropped into his chair. "Let's hear it."

But the big man did not allow Buddy to get even halfway through his explanation. Cliff interrupted, saying, "Jack Helms is a scheming, no-'count weasel. I know he's your daddy, but facts is facts."

"No objection here."

"What you got in mind?"

"I want Stanton to represent me. I can't pay him."

"You want me to bankroll you." Cliff shrugged. "I don't have no problem with that. Long as you give me my pound of flesh."

"I will agree to either work it off, or pay you back. And I'll turn down the other job offer."

"I can shake on that now, if you're ready."

"Thanks, but there's one thing more we need to discuss first." Buddy laid out the other half of his idea, feeling himself shrink as he spoke. There was so much he could have gotten wrong, and even more that might lead to his professional demise.

To his astonishment, Cliff responded with a massive grin. "That's strong, boy. Real strong."

Stanton asked, "You agree?"

"Agree? I wish I'd thought of it myself. I already got me a list of folks I need to get on the horn."

Buddy felt the balloon of fear shrink to where he could breathe easy. "So, do we have a deal?"

"Handshake work for you?"

"Absolutely." He met the CEO halfway across the desk, then asked Stanton, "Can you make time to meet my father this afternoon?"

Stanton already had his phone out. "You're sure he'll see us?"

"I spoke with his attorney on the way up. They'll be ready for us in two and a half hours."

"Give me ten minutes to rearrange a couple of matters and I'm yours."

Cliff seemed reluctant to let go of Buddy's hand. "I already like where this is going."

Buddy wished he had the confidence to reply honestly in kind. As it was, he had to make do with a single tense nod.

CHAPTER 31

When Dr. Winters called back twenty minutes later, Kimberly could scarcely believe what she was hearing. "Say again." She listened to the Hamlin official repeat himself, trying to force her brain to take it in, then declared, "I'm coming up."

"Thought you might say that."

"Can I meet you at your office?"

"Don't see why not. I have to leave at five-thirty. My youngest has a softball tournament tonight." He gave her directions and his direct number, then added, "I've got to warn you, this group you're going up against, a nest of vipers doesn't have anything on them."

"I'm not the least bit surprised," Kimberly replied. "I'm leaving now."

The two-lane highway wound its way through a fairly level cut in the Coastal Range, then entered the San Joaquin Valley. The route was mostly flat and straight and totally boring. She drove just under the speed limit and gave herself over to much-needed reflection. Because up ahead of her was a turning, and it had nothing to do with the concrete ribbon colored a dark pewter by the overcast day. She had been living by reflex for too long. It was time for a change of direction.

She was an excellent therapist. She knew that as fact. The one person she had been incapable of helping was herself. The emotional branding she had received from Jason had left her unable to trust men. Or her own judgment. She had spent the past four years pretending a hollow existence was all she could safely manage. Emphasis on the word "safe."

She was irritated by the ringing of her phone, but the read-out said it was Buddy, the one person she would allow to intrude. When she answered, Buddy said, "I'm at the clinic. And you're not."

Something told her now was not the time to discuss her findings or her journey. Not until she was certain she actually had something. "What are you doing there?"

"I'm on the way to meet with my team. Give them an update. And I'm trying to set up a meeting with my father."

He was striving for calm. However, his strain vibrated over the distance and set her gut to quivering in harmony. "How are you?" she asked.

"Not ready. I don't know if I ever will be. But I'm trying."

She listened as he described the plan he was setting in motion. Kimberly could hear his fear of the coming confrontation. His careful step-by-step approach was his way of handling what lurked around the corner.

At the same time Kimberly sensed a different emotion at work within herself, a burning glow that filled her to the point where impossible words rose from her heart to her mouth. That she was coming to care very deeply for this man. And trust him with her heart. And want to give him . . .

Everything.

She said weakly, "It's an excellent idea, Buddy."

"You really think so?"

"I do. And I like how you've brought in allies who can help you."

"That came from my time with Preston this morning. Am I wrong to tell you about what I discussed with your brother?"

"You can talk about whatever you want. Therapy is a closed door only if you want it to be. It is your decision. The important thing is that you feel safe, that you are in control."

He was silent through a pair of empty miles. Then he said, "Learning to rely on others is a challenge I've never met. I've spent my life building up my own strength, so I could take whatever came at me. Alone. I've never asked for help. I've never known what it would mean to ask somebody to . . ."

She said the words because it was either that or tell him the impossible. "To help you carry the burden. To give you strength. To shield you. To help you heal."

He drew a ragged breath. "When are you coming back?"

"I don't know yet. Tonight. Probably late."

"Will you call me?"

"Yes. All right." Kimberly cut the connection and drove holding the phone. As though she needed to maintain a physical connection to the man who was entering into combat. She breathed around the serrated regret of not having spoken the words that crowded into the car with her.

She tried to tell herself that there would be time for such things. Once they were past this hurdle. Once they were safe. But she knew the words were a myth. Because nothing about her growing feelings for Buddy Helms was safe. Starting with this trip.

CHAPTER 32

Hamlin was an old Central Valley farming town that remained firmly entrenched in a world that no longer existed. Kimberly passed a pair of strip malls, then an even larger half-empty structure called Valley Shopping. The traffic was light for early rush hour, the parking lots great seas of ribbed asphalt and rusting light towers. She followed the county official's directions and headed downtown. Hamlin's interior was a throwback to traditionalist values, sheltered by towering oaks and a quiet determination to keep moving at the slow pace of bygone days.

Kimberly parked in front of the county courthouse, a vast edifice fronting the city's main park. Kimberly followed Dr. Winters's directions around the block. She entered the south glass doors painted with the words COUNTY AND CITY above a gilded seal.

Inside the building all vestiges of grandeur were left behind. She walked a hallway of crippled marble, past endless doors of frosted glass. When the hall turned a sharp angle, she entered a reception area, where a grim-faced woman asked her to sit on an uncomfortable wooden bench. Kimberly tried to reach Buddy, but she was shunted directly to his voice mail. She called Preston, caught him between patients, and told him where she was, and why.

Her cousin replied, "Are you certifiably insane?"

"I'm doing what I think is right."

"Did you see the fear on those faces this morning when they voted down that man's dismissal notice?"

"Of course I saw."

"These are the church movers and shakers. The *church*. And they're *scared*. You should be, too. Instead, you're intending to stir the hornet's nest. Does Buddy know what you're up to?"

"No. I couldn't let him tell me not to do this."

That gave him pause. Finally Preston said, "Well, at least you're not acting on some vague whim."

"I have to go."

"Be careful, Kimmie. And call me in an hour."

She cut the connection and followed the receptionist's directions down to an open door near the end of the corridor. The man was up and moving before she arrived. Dr. Winters was in his early forties, with thinning hair and a bad suit that made him look like a lumpish bear. His face was folded into the lines of a much older man, but somehow this ungainly individual exuded a strong aura of calm. He shook her hand and nodded to her thanks and led her through a connecting steel door that jangled when he opened it. The connecting hallway was in worse shape than the one they had left, with linoleum-tiled flooring and wire cages over the ceiling lights. Most of these people wore the tan uniforms of the county sheriff's department, and they greeted Dr. Winters with easy familiarity. Her host explained, "Anytime they're called out on a possible case of juvie abuse, I play tagalong."

Winters led her into a vast office staffed by three women and a young man wearing bottle-bottom glasses, who gaped openly at Kimberly, as though some benign spirit had invaded his grim space in the guise of a roan-haired beauty. Silently a woman rose from her chair and plucked a file from a desk crammed with documents and a prehistoric computer. She was big-boned and gray-haired and eyed Kimberly with a piercing severity. Winters said simply, "Doris Hicks, Kimberly Sturgiss."

The woman walked straight past them, saying, "This way."

She led them across the hall, where she knocked on a door, checked inside, then held it open while Winters and Kimberly entered the empty conference room. "Everything I say here is off the record, are we clear on that?"

"Absolutely," Kimberly replied. "I am simply after background information."

The woman was so large she had to force herself between the arms of the chair. Her muscular bulk made her voice odd indeed, for she spoke with a high, breathless quality, like wind passing through a broken reed. "What's this all about?"

"I am counseling the wife and daughter of Jack Helms. My cousin, who works as a therapist at the same clinic, has the Helms' son as his patient."

"Where is all this happening?"

"San Luis Obispo."

She turned to the county mental-health agent and asked, "You check her out?"

"First thing, Doris. I told you that. And I know the clinic where she's working."

Doris Hicks still needed to glance over to ensure the door was shut before saying, "It's no surprise to me they're seeing you. What does shock me silly is that Jack Helms is allowing it."

"He's tried to have us fired. The people in charge vetoed his motion. Barely."

"He won't let this go." She scoped the window, then asked, "How is Jack Helms occupying himself these days?"

"He runs a local printing, advertising, and marketing company. You knew Mr. Helms?"

"Not directly. But I knew of him. Jack Helms was best buddies with the Keller boys. You ever heard of Keller Canneries?"

"I've seen the name, sure."

"The Keller clan is still the biggest landowner in this region. They hold claim to almost all the county's water rights. My daddy worked for one of the Keller rivals, a good group, paid their people a square wage and didn't shirk on benefits. That's what the unions were brought in on. Keller and their ilk were dead set against offering health insurance and retirement benefits and the like. So the unions started organizing, and the Kellers came down hard."

"I'd heard Jack Helms was used as a strikebreaker."

"You heard right. That man loved to fight. So did the Keller twins. I was thirteen years younger, so I missed most of the action. But I was the last of seven. My two older brothers learned early on to stay out of their way."

"Can you tell me what happened?"

"Don't know anything for certain. If I did, the Keller boys would have spent their life behind bars, instead of lording it over this town."

Winters spoke for the first time since sitting down. "Tell her about the riot."

"Them union boys knew sooner or later they'd have to come to this town. By then, Hamlin had gone into real estate, and built themselves the Valley Mall. Then the union started picketing. All the local movers and shakers took a giant step back. They pretended they didn't notice when Keller's strikebreakers waded in. Three men died that day. One of them was my father's best friend. Three good men."

"Jack Helms was involved?"

"I didn't say that. And don't you quote me."

"I'm not—"

Winters said, "Show her the diploma."

Doris Hicks opened the file and slid a photocopied document across the table. "Like I said, completely off the record. The Keller twins run their daddy's firm now. They basically control this town. I'm too old to go looking for another job."

Across the top of the document ran the words HAMLIN HIGH SCHOOL DIPLOMA. Beneath that was the name *Jack Helms.* Kimberly breathed a quiet "Wow."

"School records show that Jack Helms was a student there for all four of his high-school years."

"That's impossible."

"It's more than impossible," Doris Hicks said. "It's a lie. All my brothers and sisters were students at Hamlin High. I spoke with three of them. Jack Helms never set foot in that place. My oldest brother still remembers the day those Keller boys showed Jack Helms around town. Like they were all part of some great game, instead of getting ready to commit murder."

Winters said, "Now tell her the best part."

Kimberly gaped at them. "There's more?"

"Down at the bottom. Where it reads, 'School Commissioner.' That is old man Keller's signature."

"Are you sure?"

She slid another page from her file across the table. "This is his signature on a notarized document."

CHAPTER 33

"How dare that man keep us waiting!"

"It's his favorite tactic," Buddy replied. He knew Jack Helms's assistant was making note of their every word, and he did not care. "Pop relishes the chance to rattle his opponents."

"Try my patience, will he? I'll take double pleasure flaying him alive." But Stanton Parrish did not look angry. In fact, he looked positively delighted. Stanton had brought backup in the form of a court recorder and a second attorney named Melanie Evans. She was a precise, slender woman of perhaps thirty-five, who had been on the phone since entering Jack's outer office.

Stanton noticed the direction of Buddy's gaze and said, "My associate here is the finest trial attorney in the central coast. As Grady White knows, to his regret. He has gone up against Melanie twice, and both times walked away bloodied and bowed."

Buddy was coming to like Stanton Parrish immensely. But the fact did not erase his unease. Buddy knew his father. These two lawyers did not. They expected a straight fight. They expected rules. But Jack Helms was a brawler. He fought by the street code. The man who walked away breathing was the winner.

Grady White opened the door to the inner sanctum. "Buddy, who's this I see here with you, man?"

"My legal counsel."

"Don't you think you should have informed us?"

"You are so informed." But Buddy could see Grady was not surprised. Nor was he unduly concerned. Stanton Parrish took note of the same thing. And for the first time Stanton's gaze tightened in something akin to uncertainty. Which Buddy decided was not altogether a bad thing.

"Well, I guess we better move this over to the conference room, give us all a chance to take a load off. How you doing, Stanton? Melanie, nice to see you again."

But as Buddy entered the boardroom, his phone rang. He checked the readout and decided, "I need to take this."

"Buddy, man, we don't have all that much time—"

"You kept us waiting forty-five minutes," Stanton snapped. "See how you like a dose of your own medicine."

Buddy stepped into the alcove leading back to the main bull pen. "Kimberly, now isn't a good—"

"I've found it, Buddy. The smoking gun."

He stood where he was, and he listened to her rapid-fire speech, and he felt as though a filter was gradually peeled off his vision. He saw the same room he had walked through and worked in for eight long years. Only now there was a crystal clarity to the view, a vivid force that rimmed each of the worried faces looking his way. *His team.* "You're sure?"

"I held the document, Buddy. Mr. Keller, chief executive of Keller Canneries, personally signed a high-school diploma for a man who was never officially enrolled in their county's school system."

Melanie emerged from the conference room and waved in Buddy's direction. "I have to go, Kimberly. I wish I could thank you. And I will. Soon."

"I did good, didn't I?"

"You did better than that. Are you safe?"

"Of course, Buddy. I'm sitting in my car outside the sheriff's office."

"Take care. Come home. I'll call when I can." Buddy shut his phone and entered the boardroom and clamped down on everything he felt and thought. It was his common practice when entering his father's presence. Wearing the bland mask of safety. Only today he looked over and met his father's gray hurricane gaze, and thought, *Showtime*.

CHAPTER 34

Jack Helms watched his son enter with an unreadable expression. "Consorting with the enemy already. Shame on you."

Buddy settled into his seat and replied, "There are no enemies in this room."

Jack Helms merely snorted and shook his head. Stanton, on the other hand, inspected Buddy in the cautious manner of approaching a major decision. The attorney nodded once, then turned back to the room at large.

Jack Helms gave the four seated on the table's opposite side a heavy-lidded look, then demanded, "What's all this about?"

"You were the one who has brought suit against my client," Stanton responded.

"Your *client* happens to be under contract to *my firm*."

"That is simply not true, as you have already been informed."

Jack flicked his hand in dismissal. "Show them."

Grady opened a leather portfolio and withdrew a file embossed with his firm's logo. "I am sorry to inform you, sir, that you have been misled. Your client has been playing fast and loose with the truth."

Stanton cast Buddy another glance. "Is that so."

"Indeed it is." Grady's voice was overloud for the room, as though he was speaking for the courtroom he had no intention of entering. "As you will soon see."

Jack's voice carried his barely contained rage. "Won't he, Buddy. Won't he just see."

Buddy did not respond.

Grady cleared his throat and handed over the first document. "Here is a notarized copy of his original contract, dated the first of August, eight years ago. The clause regarding his noncompetition agreement is on page three. I have circled it for your convenience." He passed a second copy to Melanie, then smirked at Buddy. "I assume you don't need a copy of what you must now remember signing."

Buddy did not reply.

"Item two is an amended contract, dated four years ago. This one was also duly notarized, as you will see on the last page. Again you will find the noncompetition clause encircled on page three." He passed over two copies of a third document. "Last, but not least, we have the new contract, signed by both father and son, dated June first of last year, and again duly notarized."

Jack Helms rose to his feet and walked to the rear window. "Ring any bells, boy?"

Buddy saw no need to speak.

Grady should have looked far more satisfied than he did. "I believe that covers everything from our end. Wouldn't you agree, Jack?"

Jack Helms addressed his words to the wooded expanse bordering his grounds. "That should clarify matters for everyone concerned."

Stanton looked at his notes. The senior attorney for Hazzard Communications was clearly flummoxed. He had come prepared to move from the absence of a contract to the proposal Buddy had worked out. Buddy's idea was to forge a merger between the Helms Group and Hazzard's much larger company. A genteel acquisition—with Jack Helms offered a position on the board as a means of smoothing his transition to retirement. Two old foes working in tandem. Facing a new business climate in the best possible manner. United. Strong enough to overcome whatever uncertainty tomorrow might bring. Instead, Jack Helms had blindsided them.

Buddy could almost watch the attorney's mind at work. Stanton Parrish had to decide whether his new client was lying. If he was, Stanton's position on the Hazzard board meant disavowing himself of everything to do with Buddy Helms.

Regardless of whether the documents were valid, either way Stanton could not in good faith broach the possibility of a merger. Either the father or the son was lying. Both options negated Buddy's concept. Buddy could not blame the attorney for hunting down the nearest exit.

But he could hope.

Buddy had long suspected his father intended something like this. Jack Helms was infamous for plying havoc with a blade his opponents did not notice until it was sticking between their ribs. Buddy was not surprised. Saddened, yes. Filled with bitter regret, most definitely. And also a bit ashamed.

"I think we're all done here." Stanton slapped his own folder shut. "For the record I am only coming to know my client. But I, for one, am convinced that what my client told me prior to arriving here is the truth. Buddy Helms has never been issued a formal contract with this company. There is no valid noncompete clause. He is free as a bird."

Grady White did a fair job of generating indignation. "Are you accusing my client of willfully misleading an officer of the court?"

"Someone in the room most certainly did. Yes."

"Sir, I will have you up on charges of slander."

"That is certainly one option." Stanton shifted in his chair. "Coming, Buddy?"

"Not just yet."

But before he could speak, his father's cell phone rang. Jack glanced at the readout, then stalked from the room. Buddy knew Stanton wanted to treat this as an affront and depart as well. But Buddy had not yet twisted the dragon's tail.

Even so, as he waited for his father to return, Buddy felt his mother's presence like a physical force. It granted him a distance both from the tension and the people, enabling him to see what his mother would have labeled as the right way forward.

Jack Helms reentered the conference room and pretended to be surprised. "You're still here?"

Stanton started to offer a rejoinder, but Buddy halted him before the words were uttered. "It doesn't have to be like this, Pop."

His father snorted softly and returned to his position by the window.

Buddy went on, "I grew up thinking you were the finest man on earth. I'm asking you to let that part of you live again. Mom wants—"

Jack Helms addressed his words to the window. "You leave your mother out of this."

Buddy accepted that his words were probably futile. But glad he had said them nonetheless. "I'm leaving the firm. I have an idea that I think would give us a peaceful resolution. But for this to work, I need you to drop this charade and treat me as someone who has your best interests at heart."

Jack Helms turned slowly. For the first time in what felt like years, there was a fractured indecision to how Jack looked at him. As though his father was uncertain who he was, or who spoke to him. "You want a peaceful resolution? You stop this nonsense and come back where you belong."

Buddy nodded slowly, the motion carrying through his entire body. Knowing that the decision was Jack's. Not his.

As his father started for the exit, Buddy asked, "What is your connection to Keller Canneries?"

His father froze in midstride. "My clients have no place in this room."

"For the record, the Keller family's business empire formed the basis upon which the Helms Group was founded." Buddy had always loathed those early advertising accounts. They shrieked of staid conservatism. The actors who stood before those perfectly lit stoves smiled like performers on an old Art Linkletter show, all teeth and no spirit. The perfect kitchens filled with perfect people. Year after year his father and the Keller twins met and laughed and ate aged prime rib at the Gold Rush Steakhouse. Buddy had endured too many wasted hours working on projects as confining as coffins. "Don't make me do this, Pop."

His father did not respond.

"If you force me to take one more step, we'll be discussing Hamlin. And your actions for the Keller family. Before you went to UC Davis."

Jack Helms glided back over to loom above the table. "Don't go messing where you don't belong, boy. We're discussing your job."

"There is no job. I've left the company."

He stabbed the papers in front of Grady. "This says otherwise."

"We both know that contract is a total fabrication."

"Wrong." He stabbed them again. "We both know you've lost."

Buddy turned to Stanton. "For the record there were more than two dozen firms like Keller that formed the Helms Group's financial backbone. Canneries, Central Valley grocery chains, regional department stores. But the stores have mostly been sold out to national groups with in-house marketing teams. These new conglomerates shoot their own catalogue and layouts. The remaining clients aren't enough to keep the Helms Group afloat."

"I'm a busy man," Jack Helms snapped. "I've got a whole company of people to run. And you're a misguided boy whose wasting a passel of important people's time."

"Either you'll be put on the stand, or I will. And my attorneys will ask questions you don't want to hear. About how you got into UC Davis using a high-school certificate from a county where you never resided." Buddy gave his father a chance to respond, then went on, "But you did go there, didn't you? To Hamlin. Old man Keller brought you in when the unions came to Hamlin. Didn't he? And you did something for him. Didn't you, Pop? Something so great—"

Jack Helms underwent a subtle transformation. The uncertainty did not so much vanish as become overlaid by a varnish. His gaze grew flat, his voice softly frigid. "You stop right there."

"Something so important, Mr. Keller himself signed your graduation certificate. Which he could, since he was the superintendent of schools. Old man Keller falsified county documents, which state you attended all four years of high school there. But you didn't. You couldn't have. You were seventeen when you first showed up in Hamlin. It was summer. That autumn you entered UC Davis as a freshman—"

"This is none of your affair."

"You've made it my affair, Pop." Buddy stopped for a moment. Not out of uncertainty. Rather, he was increasingly convinced his father already knew what he was going to say. Jack's protests were almost a rote declaration, the sort of response that was given only because one was expected. Buddy pressed on, "But it's not the high-school documents that are important, are they? Or how Keller set you up here in San Luis Obispo when you graduated. It was what you did on the night of the Hamlin riots, isn't it? When three good men went down. Three good men."

Jack Helms rose to his feet and gave a tight smile. "All right, that's enough."

Buddy rose as well. He knew his father was planning something more. A counterattack so powerful Jack Helms expected it to crush and overwhelm. But as he stood there, staring across the table, Buddy grew increasingly certain of two things. The first was, he could survive whatever Jack had intended. The second certainty he spoke out loud. "I'm free, Pop. I'm not coming back. Not for a day. Not for an hour. Accept this and move on. Otherwise I'll bring all this out into the light of day."

Jack Helms continued to offer his mirthless smile. "You're nothing, and you never will be."

"You're wrong about that as well." He gestured to the attorneys on his side of the table. "We're done here."

CHAPTER 35

"You should have shared that information before we entered into negotiations," Stanton Parrish chided.

"I didn't have it to share," Buddy replied.

"That phone call you received as we were entering?"

Buddy nodded. "A friend traveled to Hamlin. I didn't even know she was going."

"She should have told you." But there was no heat to Stanton's riposte. Indeed, the man seemed positively giddy. "I would have rewritten the morning with that tune. Oh, my, yes. I would have invited the buffoon to disembowel himself so we could feast upon his innards."

Melanie coughed discreetly. Stanton gathered himself and took a step back from the drama he had missed. "I do beg your pardon. That was most indiscreet."

"I can't thank you enough," Buddy replied. "Both of you."

"I can still hardly bring myself to believe the man actually went so far as to present falsified documents to an officer of the court."

"Falsified and notarized," Melanie added.

"And you believed me," Buddy said.

"You are our client," Stanton replied. "It's our business to accept your word as legitimate."

"You went far beyond that."

"As we should have." Stanton inspected his young client. "I would have expected a good deal more satisfaction on your part. You have all but won the day."

"There's no way they'll take this to court," Melanie agreed. "I would bring Grady White up on charges before the bar."

Buddy shook his head. The court was never the issue. "Pop's not done here."

"What possibly could he do at this point?"

"I don't know. But my gut tells me . . ." When he went silent, they waited with the patience of trusting companions. He finished, "When I started working here, Pop often claimed he never lost a fight. He walked away from some. But he never lost." It was a declaration that had always brought Jack Helms grim joy. Buddy glanced back at the empty boardroom window. "My father won't walk away from this one. He can't."

"Well, it is my duty as your attorney to announce that Jack Helms has . . ."

Buddy's phone rang. He checked the readout, excused himself, and walked over to stand beneath the flapping flags. "Kimberly?"

"Buddy, oh, Buddy."

There was a muffled quality to her voice, as though she was talking around a lump of cotton. All his fear and his worry coagulated into a dagger of ice that plunged deep into his gut. "What's happened?"

Kimberly had difficulty shaping the words. "I want to say how much I—"

There was a squeal of painful protest, a rustling sound. Buddy yelled, *"Kimberly!"*

A deep male voice demanded, "Who am I speaking with?"

"Put Kimberly on the line!"

"This is Sheriff Hinkle of Hamlin County. I need to know who I'm talking with here."

"Buddy. Buddy Helms."

"Mr. Helms, your associate here—wait, Jim, give me that ID. Okay. Ms. Kimberly Sturgiss has been involved in a serious road incident. She is being arrested on charges of reckless driving, driving under the influence, and reckless endangerment."

"No, that's not—"

"She struck a sheriff's car, son. The lady is going down."

Buddy glanced back at the building behind him. A shadow drifted across the boardroom windows. There, and then gone with spectral ease.

"Mr. Helms, you still there?"

"I'm here."

"There's a message I've been asked to pass on by some folks down here." The sheriff spoke with a casual brutality. The voice of a professional interrogator. A man used to being feared. "We take care of our own."

CHAPTER 36

Kimberly touched her lip with her tongue and tasted blood. The left side of her face was painfully swollen where she had struck the car's side window. Her shoulder was severely bruised but thankfully not dislocated. Her forehead had finally stopped bleeding. Her lip was inflamed and one tooth was loose. Her left eye was almost completely shut. She heard the men move in the jail's central office, out beyond the electric doors. She knew she should be terrified. These men assumed they held all the cards. They had been allied to the power in this county for so long, they could not even imagine someone threatening their domain. Instead, she felt strangely calm. She hoped it was not some false peace drawn from an undiagnosed concussion. She didn't think so. But she couldn't be certain.

She had been brought straight here from the accident site. Her only visitor had been a pair of men dressed in matching black suits and white shirts. No ties. Their hair was slicked down with so much oil their heads glistened like wavy mirrors. They eyed her with the calmness of reptiles. She knew that gaze. She had endured the same look from Buddy's father.

"She don't look like much," the one on the right said.

The sheriff was bulky in the manner of an aging boxer, big and strong, with scarred hands that were settled comfortably atop his broad belt. "She got the wind knocked out of her, that's for certain."

"She seen the doc?"

"Nah, she don't need no doctor. Do you, honey?"

The man on the right must have been the twins' appointed spokesman. "You've seen your share of bad drivers and folks who don't know better than to fall down stairs. Haven't you, Sheriff?"

"I have, and that's a fact." The sheriff did not so much take pleasure from her pain as simply not care. "Enough to know when one don't need the doc."

The old man pulled out an old-fashioned pocket watch. "When is Jack due?"

"He'll be here sometime this evening."

"You sure she called the Helms kid?"

"She surely did. And she said her bit. Then I spoke to him myself." The sheriff's smile was the worst part about him. "Jack's boy screamed like a stuck pig."

"What do you aim on doing with the kid?"

"Not much. Give him a good look and the choice of doing what his pappy says or watching her pay for his mistakes." He gestured at the door. "Y'all don't have to hang around for this."

"Yes, we do. Debts like this need to be paid in person." The man snapped his watch shut. "How long does Jack figure the boy'll mind him?"

"The old man only needs him for a while. Got to nail down some deal." The sheriff shrugged his unconcern. "After that, Jack says the boy can crawl away if he wants. Most times, though, once they're good and licked, they stay that way. These young folks just don't have much backbone."

The man on the left spoke for the first time. Only when the words emerged in a rattling wheeze did Kimberly notice the scar that ran over his Adam's apple. "That ain't the question we need to be asking. What are we gonna do about our leak?"

"I had myself a good old talk with that pair," the sheriff replied. "You ain't gonna hear another peep outta them. They like living too much."

"And the documents?"

The sheriff showed his easy, vacant grin. "What documents are those?"

Only when they moved away did Kimberly realize she had been holding her breath.

The women's holding pen was a cage that was barred on top as well as sides. Mold-covered plywood walls offered privacy around the washroom. The cage was held inside a larger room that looked like it might once have been an auditorium. The former stage held a glassed-in observation chamber. The men's area was probably behind a whitewashed wall to the left of her bunk. Four interview rooms with steel doors lined the opposite wall. Kimberly could not look at them without shivering. She did not hear any screams. She did not see any other prisoners. But the solitude offered her no comfort, nor any sense of hope that she might be spared. She thought of Buddy entering into this heartless domain, and enduring his own brand of casual brutality. Tears leaked from her good eye.

They had laid their trap well. She had just left the Hamlin town limits and her car had not yet reached cruising speed, when the sheriff's car had emerged from behind a broken-down wall and jumped over the grassy verge. The lone officer had not appeared to be watching her at all. Instead, he spoke into the car's microphone and scouted in both directions. Then just as she passed, he gunned the motor. Taking aim. At her.

He smashed her front left fender and the driver's door. He gunned his motor, allowing her momentum to carry them both off the road. Kimberly was rammed nose-first into the drainage ditch.

She must have blacked out, because the next thing she knew,

the sheriff was reaching across her, pulling out her purse. The move had made no sense. Her brain felt as matted as her hair and as inflamed as her face. The sheriff didn't even glance her way until she moaned out what she hoped was a plea for help. "You just hold your horses, missy. I'll be getting to you soon enough."

Then he pulled out her phone, plucked a piece of paper from his shirt pocket, punched in a number, waited a second, then held the phone to her ear and said, "You just tell the Helms boy he needs to come and get it."

CHAPTER 37

They gathered at Beth's apartment. Buddy wanted to race off, play the Don Quixote of San Luis Obispo, tilt his meager lance at all the windmills. But despite his rage, he remained clear-headed enough to name his goals. He was not after chivalry in solitary battle. He was after bringing his lady home.

Yet the waves of rage continued to crash inside him. So he set his headquarters up where a woman who had spent years maintaining an impossible peace in the face of intolerable storms could calm his spirit and focus his mind.

He placed the calls. He reached out to those he could trust, and asked for the help that a life depended upon. Actually, two lives.

Stanton Parrish and Melanie Evans made a valiant tactical team. Buddy listened to them plot and phone and talk and plead, and knew they were doing all that was possible on that score. Which meant he was ready when the call he had been waiting for came through. He waved as Cliff Hazzard rose from his Rolls, and turned away. "This is Buddy."

"Grady White here, old buddy. How you doing?"

"What do you want, Grady?"

"I'm just calling, you know, to ask if you could do the right thing here."

The rage surged and roiled, but he held it down tight. " 'The right thing.' "

"Sure. The future of your father's company is on the line here."

"That's right, Grady. It is."

"Your own father. Shouldn't you at least give him—"

"What are the terms?"

"Same as before. Nothing's changed. He wants you back. Isn't that what matters here? You've still got a home at the Helms Group."

The longer he clamped down on everything he had spent a lifetime not saying, the easier his rage resided, down deep where it could not dominate. Down where it crystallized his thinking, kept him from raging at a flaccid little messenger boy. "I am going to counter."

"You . . . What?"

"I need some time to work things through." Buddy checked his watch. "It's just turned six. I'll phone you by nine. Give me a number where I can reach you."

"Buddy, man, I'm not sure—"

"Give me a number, Grady."

Buddy listened to the attorney rattle off a number, but did not bother to write it down. He just said, "Three hours." And hung up.

Cliff Hazzard observed the exchange with a slit-eyed smile. "Jack Helms ain't waiting any three hours."

"No."

"So, what are you going to do?"

"The only thing I can do," Buddy replied. "Hurry."

Cliff kissed Beth's cheek. "What on earth are you doing, Miss Beth, living in this rat hole?"

"This is where I am meant to be, Cliff. And it suits me just fine."

Cliff Hazzard studied her intently. Buddy saw what the older man did. His mother did not look good. Cliff demanded, "What does Jack have to say about your new digs?"

"I did not ask his opinion."

"Bet he didn't like being kept out of that loop, not one tiny bit."

"I did not ask him that, either," Beth replied. "Coffee?"

Their numbers grew with exponential swiftness. Preston arrived two minutes after Cliff. He was accompanied by the senior pastor, Ross Burridge. Buddy had waited for them to arrive to detail his idea. But telling them directly ran the risk of his plan being sidelined. Preston's fury was just begging for a reason to explode. And Cliff Hazzard had started talking about taking in an army before he even knew what the target was.

So Buddy called the one man not present who was crucial to his plan. By then, their numbers had grown to where they spilled out over the patio's edges and down into the lawn. Buddy raised his voice to where they could all hear, then had to explain to Mark Weathers why he was yelling. The CEO of the Santa Barbara software group took it in, and demanded, "Cliff Hazzard is there?"

"Standing right beside me."

"Will he confirm that he agrees with your offer?"

Cliff Hazzard took the phone and said, "I agree with everything young Helms just said, including the parts I don't understand. Do this deal, and Buddy and his group will run the first year of your marketing campaign for cost."

Cliff listened a moment longer, then said, "Because if we had it my way, we'd be heading off to war. And that won't do us any good at all, unless we were out to ruin some young lives, including the lady they got holed up in the Hamlin jail." He grinned at Buddy and added, "Besides which, I've taken a shine to young Helms here. To sign him onto my team, I've got to make this work. And I'm coming to trust the boy with a lot more than promo copy."

Buddy took back the phone and tried to find some way to thank Cliff. But all he could think of was the team of watchful faces. Trusting him to make the right move. Waiting for him to point the way. *His team.*

Cliff said, "The man is waiting."

Buddy turned to Preston. "You agree with this?"

"Personally, I'd like to take your father hostage and offer them a trade," Preston said.

"Won't work."

"Then I'd go for unlocking Mr. Hazzard's gun cabinet and waking up the world."

"Tempting," Buddy said. "But it would doom your cousin."

Preston shrugged. "Then I agree."

Buddy lifted the phone and asked Mark Weathers, "Are you in?"

"You're certain there's no way I can up Hazzard's offer and have you come join our team?"

"I am grateful," Buddy replied. "But no."

The software executive accepted the news with a sigh. "Give me a call in an hour. We'll try and have something mapped out by then."

As they loaded up, the senior pastor was the last to leave the veranda. Buddy assumed he was having second thoughts over becoming further involved. But when he approached Ross Burridge, Buddy realized the man was arguing into his phone. He heard the pastor say, "Because we've spent too long being afraid of this man. Because what he has condoned is not merely illegal, it is against God's law. Because we have to make a stand. Because we have to take our position on the side of right and truth! Does that answer your question?" Ross Burridge slapped the phone shut. "I've been waiting years to say that. Too long."

Beth asked, "Are they coming?"

"That's between them and their God."

Buddy braced for an argument and turned to his mother. But before he could insist that she not come along, Beth announced, "Carey and I will stay here."

He noticed for the first time the way his sister's gaze had become inwardly focused, as though she had already removed herself from the fray. He saw the two women exchange a glance, and resisted the urge to ask what was going on. He hugged them both, and breathed one strong breath with each. All the words just had to wait.

They made for a motley armada. Stanton Parrish drove Cliff Hazzard's Rolls, both men working the phones before they pulled from the drive. The pastor and his team drove a Lincoln. Buddy's group from work was there in full force, right down to the secretaries, crammed into a boxy Ion and two Ford Escapes. As Buddy started toward Preston's vintage Mercedes, the old man called from the patio, "Son!"

"Sir?"

Josiah motioned with one arthritic hand. Reluctantly Buddy climbed the stairs again. When Buddy closed the distance, the old man said, "I marched with Martin Luther King. I crossed two states on my feet. Fighting the good fight. Standing up for them who were too afraid or been silenced too long. Reminding them what it meant to have a voice."

Buddy had no idea what to say to that.

The old man nodded his approval to Buddy's response. "You go take your stand with open hands, boy. Know there's a rightness to answering their weapons with nothing but a message of peace. Their day is over. They just don't know it yet." His nods were strong enough to set the rocker to creaking. "Your mother and I'll be here waiting when the battle's won."

CHAPTER 38

It could have been a hard journey for Beth and Carey both, pushing through the night on a mission most would have called hopeless from the start. But Beth was filled with a remarkable sense of peace, as though they served as divine messengers. Even here, in the midst of man-made chaos, there was a unique rightness to each breath.

When they pulled up to a stoplight, Carey glanced over at Beth. A passing streetlight illuminated the way her mother was partially curled up in her seat, using the door for support.

"Are you sure you're up for this, Momma?"

"I wouldn't miss this for the world."

"You don't look good. Do you have your pain medication?"

"In my pocket. Where it's staying until this is done." Beth met her daughter's gaze. "Now isn't the time to be concerned about me."

They used the house directly across the street as their way station. Beth knew the owners spent their winters in Arizona with their son's family. She had a key to their home, which she probably should return. Beth was friends with all her former neighbors. Beth also assumed they shared a unified response to news she had left Jack: *Finally.*

When Carey pulled into the drive, Beth told her daughter, "I'm so proud of you."

Carey cut the engine and turned in her seat. "Why would you say such a thing?"

"Because it's true."

"I've made a mess out of my life. I fell in love with the wrong men and pretended I could make it right."

"You refused to let your father crush the child in you. In your own way you are a very strong and capable young woman."

Carey's eyes shone bright in passing headlights. "You've never told me that before."

"Which is my mistake." Beth reached over and touched her daughter's cheek. She wanted to say that if it were possible to pine for someone from the grave, Beth would miss her baby girl most of all. But now was most certainly not the time for maudlin tears.

Carey stared across the street at her former home. "I can't believe I'm about to go ask my father to do the impossible."

"Two things, sweetheart, and I want you to listen very carefully. First, the important thing here is that we try. Second, it's impossible only if Jack insists on holding to a course I know, deep as my own bones, that Jack already realizes is wrong."

Her husband chose that moment to pull down the street and into the drive. As the garage door cranked open, a pain momentarily seized Beth, which was bad, but it fled as swiftly as it had arrived.

"Are you all right, Momma?"

"I'm fine." The boundaries of her world were growing smaller by the hour. "Come around and help me, please."

Beth entered the house, supported by her daughter. Upstairs, Fox News blared from the television in their bedroom. Jack followed a nightly routine, going straight into the shower with the news turned up high enough for him to hear it over the water.

Carey's breathing was audible, tight little gasps that were a fraction of an inch off moans. Beth wanted to tell her it was all going to be just fine. But she would not taint this night with a lie.

Then the television cut off and a heavy tread emerged from the bedroom and started down the upstairs hall. Carey's grip tightened to where it pained Beth.

As prepared as she thought she was, watching Jack come down the stairs was a shock. Her husband wore a suit she had never seen before, three-piece and black and creased from having been stored away for a long time, perhaps even decades. He wore a starched white shirt buttoned to his neck, and no tie. He froze on the middle step, clearly astonished by their appearance. "What on earth?"

"I was about to ask you the same thing." She pointed at his attire and said the first thing that came to her mind. "You're wearing clothes from your darkest hour."

"Beth, I . . ."

"Is that a proper way for you to go meet with your son? *Our* son, Jack?"

"He's gone against me." But her presence had rattled him in an unexpected fashion. Beth could see it in his gaze.

"Tell me something, Jack. Do you even remember the day we met? How you begged my grandfather to stop his revival and take you down and baptize you? How you pleaded with him when he asked you to wait until the lakeside service that night? Do you remember the words you spoke?"

He stared at her, then Carey, then back again. He did not move from the middle stair, as though their presence trapped him.

"Do you remember, Jack? How you screamed the words there in front of everybody? What did you say?"

Her daughter had turned to her as well. Hearing these things for the very first time.

"You told my grandfather, 'I've got blood on my hands.' And what did Granddaddy do, Jack? He walked you down to the lake's shore and he dipped you in the water. And what did you do, Jack? Do you even remember? You wept. You cried like a little child."

Beth was weeping now, and she heard Carey's half-formed sob. But the tears weren't important. The only thing that mattered was how her husband remained there. Mouth agape. Listening.

"*That* is the man I married, Jack. *That* is the man I'm asking you to be once more." She shook her hand at him. "Not this man who drapes himself in old shadows and goes off to do wrong. And that's the only way to describe what you've set in motion, whatever it is. A dark and dreadful wrongness."

She stopped then because the pain struck, as though she needed the punctuation mark to halt her. She held herself erect by will alone, and took one tight breath after another.

"Daddy?" Carey's voice was little-girl small. But it came out clear enough to cause her father's gaze to swivel around. "Something's come to me during therapy that I want to share with you."

Her father wanted to sweep it away as garbage. But the motion died before it was formed, a mere toss of his left wrist, a grimace, and neither truly felt. Jack stood. He waited. He *listened.*

Carey went on, "I remembered something I had forgotten or just put away. That's a big part of therapy for me, dealing with memories. I remembered how it was when Sylvie went at you like she did. And how it brought out . . ."

"The shadows," Beth offered quietly.

"Right. The thing is, the reason I'm here, I want to be the *other* daughter. The one who helps bring you *back* to us."

Beth's breath caught up sharp, but this time it was because her heart was pierced by joy. "Carey, that is so beautiful."

Her daughter glanced over. "I've been thinking about that

ever since you asked me to come tonight. How I want to be the daughter who helps heal away the scars."

He took a shuddering breath. And tried to push them away with the words "I need to be going."

"Go where, Jack? Away from your wife and your daughter?"

"You were the one who left me."

"And look where it's brought us." She felt an immense calm settle upon her, a rightness that flooded her with a force so powerful she knew he was going to agree before she spoke the words that had come to her in the car. She *knew* this. "Jack, look at me. No, I want you to really *look*. Do you see it, Jack? I'm leaving this earth. It's only a matter of weeks now, maybe even days."

"Oh, Momma . . ."

"Shush, child, I'm speaking to your father." Beth waited through another hard breath. "Jack, you're the only man I've ever loved. And without you there beside me, heaven is going to be a lonely place."

Carey collapsed. She fell to her knees there in the front hall, and she sobbed. Beth rested a hand upon her daughter's head, stroking the child she loved more than life. Then she reached out her free hand and she said, "Turn away from those shadows, Jack. They're not you, and they don't own you. Come back to me and your family. While there's still time."

CHAPTER 39

Buddy Helms approached the Hamlin Courthouse through the park. The clouds had rolled back, and the Central Valley was enjoying a splendid night. The moon fashioned a silvery carpet as he stepped forward. Buddy walked alone because he had said it needed to be done this way. The growing number of people who had joined him disliked the idea, but they had relented. Mostly because their leaders, Preston and Stanton and Cliff and Ross and Bernard, had granted him silent agreement. So he started through the last line of elms, armed only with the phone in his right hand.

But as he started to emerge, a phone sounded from up ahead. The sheriff lounged on the top stair with a pair of aging scarecrows. Their dark suits and narrow expressions were drawn from a bygone era. Several uniformed deputies lounged a couple of stairs lower. They all watched as the sheriff lifted his phone and said, "Jack, where you at?"

The night held its breath as the sheriff angled his body around, his thick leather belt creaking as he turned to the two dark-suited men and said, "What you mean, you ain't coming?"

One of the old men tromped forward, hand outstretched. "Give me that." He wrenched the phone from the sheriff and said, "We're here on account of you and that debt. Now I want . . ." The old man's voice did not so much cut off as grind down, reduced to ashes by whatever he heard. The hand retreated slowly from his face. "Jack hung up on me."

Buddy took that as the only sign he was likely to get that evening, and stepped through the trees and down into the street.

"That's far enough!" Despite the night's unexpected change of direction, the sheriff's voice carried stern authority. "You the Helms boy?"

"That's right."

"What took you so long?" He gestured to the two silent wraiths. But the motion carried the same sense of uncertainty as his voice. "You kept your betters waiting. They don't like tardiness. You're gonna have to pay."

"Let Kimberly go, and we'll leave," Buddy said. "No foul, no penalty."

"Boy, you must think you're still out there on the coast. This here is our town. You done stuck your lady's hand in a whole mess of trouble." The sheriff and his deputies started down toward him. "And you're gonna rue the day."

Buddy raised his voice and yelled, *"Now!"*

The sight of all those men and women appearing through the trees must have been something. But Buddy could not risk looking. He kept his gaze steady upon the sheriff, who faltered for a second time. "Y'all get on about your business!"

"That is *exactly* what we're doing!" Cliff Hazzard shouted back. "This young man is all *about* my business."

"This is an unlawful assembly! Move or we'll . . ."

He stopped when the two news crews came into view. Cliff Hazzard's press team had done their job well. Fresno was the closest city to possess a television station of its own, and to have two show up on such short notice was a remarkable feat.

Cliff yelled, "Smile, why don't you, Sheriff! You're going out live at eleven!"

The sheriff barked at his deputies, "Clear that group out of here!"

While the officers' attention was elsewhere, Buddy lifted his phone and said, "Go. Repeat, *go.*"

For an instant nothing happened. Then bedlam erupted in front of him.

Every light in the courthouse blazed on. Every siren whooped. The lights went off again. Then on. Now they flickered, slow at first, then faster and faster, flashing like manic Christmas lights. The police siren and the fire alarm and the door alarms yelped in unison, all forty-three of them. Buddy knew the number because one of Mark Weathers's top software engineers had hacked the courthouse system before he and Cliff Hazzard and Preston had entered the Hamlin city limits. Weathers had tried to hide his humor behind weary resignation as he had explained how most of the truly gifted software engineers were hackers at heart. His team had shown a childlike delight at taking over the Hamlin Courthouse's system. On company time.

The building also possessed a massive PA system, intended to supplant regular communications in an emergency. Which Buddy figured the sheriff and his deputies, by now, agreed this most definitely was. From all-weather speakers embedded in the high concrete eaves came a blast of electro-rock and the banshee wail of youths screaming that it was time to freak the system.

The sheriff had his pistol out, but the television lights competed with the courthouse's strobe effect. The music overwhelmed anything he might have been trying to say.

Which was when every electronic-controlled door in the entire courthouse sprang wide open.

Buddy decided now was as good a time as any to mosey on inside.

He was midway up the main stairs when Preston bounded up beside him. The music had switched to an electro-punk version of the old Beatles song, inviting the world to relax and float gently downstream. Preston shouted something Buddy did not need to understand, and then together they passed through the main entrance.

One of the television crews had opted to join them, which was probably why none of the deputies impeded their progress down the hallway. They followed the map the hackers had kindly supplied, compliments of county records.

Their good humor was erased, however, when they entered the women's wing and found Kimberly inside the cage. Preston wept and shouted his defiance at a pair of bulky officers who tried to stop them. Buddy did not trust himself to speak at all. He merely hefted the wounded lady and carried her out.

Kimberly hid her face in his neck, for his every step was marked by the television lights. Buddy knew his rage showed, as did Preston's angry tears. And he decided that there was no reason why one of his precious team should not weep over the casual cruelty of life's uncaring hand.

Buddy carried her back outside, past the furious sheriff. He did not release her, not even when the pastor reached out for her, not even as he slipped into the Rolls's rear seat. Nor did he speak, for he would not permit the evening to be lashed by a rage he could scarcely keep inside. He would not foul this night or his life by taking his father's course, and releasing the molten force that would most certainly wound friend and foe and family alike. No, his was a different compass heading. Buddy showed the gentler choice he had made by the way he cradled his newly beloved, and stroked her hair away from the damaged cheek, and watched the fetid stench of Hamlin vanish behind them, and let Kimberly sink into the mercy of sleep.

CHAPTER 40

Buddy woke twice in the night, chased into wakefulness by the monster's roar. He lay on his makeshift pallet and stared about him, both times unable to remember at first where he was, or why. Then he heard the breath of uneasy slumber from the next room, and it all became clear.

Both times he stepped to the open doorway leading to Kimberly's chamber. He stared down at the form on the bed. The moon was not quite full, but it fell strong and silver through the window. He saw the sheen of perspiration on her damaged face. Buddy felt the invitation to rage at the monster who had managed to creep from his nightmares and invade his world. But he refused to give in.

The next morning he borrowed running gear from Preston, who offered them with the ease of a man who was genuinely happy with his company. Buddy ran the alien streets beneath maple and oak and pine. He made mental note of the more attractive lanes. He jogged and he looked and he wondered if this was how it meant to redefine his own boundaries.

Kimberly was up when he returned. She lifted her face, and

Buddy realized she was inviting him to kiss her undamaged side. Preston got off the phone and announced that he had not been able to make a doctor's appointment until that afternoon. Buddy told her, "You should go back to sleep."

"Another hour or so won't make any difference." She eyed him above the border of her mug. "Thank you for staying over last night."

"You asked."

"That's right. I did. How was your bed?"

"He didn't have a bed," Preston said. "He didn't want one."

"It was fine," Buddy replied. "I often sleep on the floor."

"You told me that last night." She set down her mug and reached for his hand. "You told me a lot of things."

Buddy colored, mostly at how Preston smiled at the two of them. "I thought you were asleep."

"I was, until I realized what you were whispering. Then I made myself stay awake." She slipped her second hand atop his. "You can tell me again, now if you want. Just to make sure I didn't miss anything."

Preston cleared his throat. "I think this is the point when I pretend I need to be heading to the office."

Before Buddy could come up with a decent response, the house phone rang. Preston answered, then held it out. "It's for Buddy."

He took the receiver, and afterward it seemed as though he had known what was to be spoken even before the words emerged. As though some ethereal force invaded his peace before he held the phone.

A tearful Carey said, "Pop's housekeeper found him on the kitchen floor and called an ambulance. He's suffered a stroke."

Buddy found himself mildly grateful over how his sister could weep for them both this morning. But all he said was "I'll be right over."

"Wait, Buddy, there's more." And with a heart far more broken than her voice, she delivered the morning's real news.

CHAPTER 41

Six days later, they moved Jack Helms by ambulance from the regional hospital into the hospice care center at Moondust Lake. Beth already resided there. Buddy traveled up in the ambulance, accompanied by his sister.

Carey bore the bruised creases of too many sleepless nights. Buddy assumed he looked pretty much the same.

Kimberly was waiting for them when they arrived at Moondust Lake. By this point her presence had become a natural component of his life. She had molded herself into his routine of tragic responsibilities, and done so willingly. Her face was wreathed in the rainbow of healing bruises. Several times each day Buddy endured the tight gazes of nurses who assumed he was the one responsible, and who accepted Kimberly's explanation of a car accident with bad grace. But their lives were so full, they could not afford to give much room or concern to such suspicions.

On the ninth day Buddy worked out a routine so that they could all spend time with the afflicted while granting each of them space to resume their normal lives. They had to. The world was turning, and it did not appear that either parent would be going home. Ever.

There were moments when it all became too much for him to bear. Buddy had never known such weakness, or perhaps never allowed himself to feel it before. He had to struggle at times with futile rage. He became angry with Carey for not having insisted on telling him about Beth's illness the moment she learned. He was furious with his mother for dying. He was maddest of all at himself for not having delved further into the changes he had noticed, and been there, and done something.

But he was also learning to grow through the pain, thanks mostly to Kimberly. He had listened to her patient explanations, time and again, and heard beyond the words that here was a woman he could trust to help him reknit his world. Once the passage was endured, and the tragedy borne, and the future again became something other than a container for bleakness.

And then there was the most remarkable turning of all. Five times he asked Carey to relive the confrontation with their father. The words she and their mother spoke. The reaction of their father. How Jack had wept there in the front foyer with his wife and daughter. And apologized. And begged their forgiveness. And then called the shadow folk in Hamlin. And expressed to them what Beth said was necessary. Word for word.

On the eleventh day Buddy arrived for what had become his regular evening vigil. There was a great deal he shared with his inert father during these hours. How the Helms Group's board of directors had named him acting CEO, the only way possible to salvage the Lexington account. How Cliff Hazzard's company was in the process of absorbing the Helms Group. How the merger documents had been finalized and approved by both boards. How the Helms Group would become Hazzard's new marketing powerhouse. How Buddy was to become the group's managing director, answering directly to Cliff Hazzard and the board. How Buddy was seeing Kimberly on a regular basis. How he was learning a new meaning to the word "love." Almost every day.

And how Jack's wife of thirty-seven years was in the next room. Lying in a bed from which she would never emerge. Not in this life.

Sometimes Carey joined him. When she did, they talked together, trying to restore a fragment of the family that had almost been destroyed. Buddy almost always wept in those moments. But he had come to understand that there was nothing in the world wrong with a few tears.

Tonight he was in there alone, for Kimberly and Carey had gone out to the airport to greet Sylvie and bring her back. Buddy did not mention his sister's arrival. Sylvie had claimed she was only back to see her mother. He and Carey had spent hours on the phone, urging Sylvie to reconsider her stand regarding Jack.

Buddy seated himself by the bed and began relating the news about his day. The nurse came and checked Jack's vitals and smiled down at Buddy as she departed. Showing approval for the son who sought to strengthen the familial bond. While he still had time.

Beth lay comforted by far more than the drugs they fed steadily into her arm. Her room was situated next to Jack's, at her request. The people here were very discreet, which was hardly remarkable for a place that dealt in closure. They were also utterly unflappable. Beth had accepted the news that the hospice only had one double room, and it was occupied. She responded by asking if she might have just the one wall separating her from her husband. The staff responded with placid geniality. It was her departure, to shape as she wished. Beth could not have found a more agreeable setting if she had designed it herself.

She heard Buddy's voice through both the wall and her open

door. She did not need to understand the words. Days back, he and Carey had told her what they intended. She had responded that she was proud of them, and they were doing the right thing, and for the right reason. Drawing a healing peace into their relationship with Jack. At long last.

Beth listened to her son's steady drone, and felt a sudden shift inside herself, as though some binding cord had just been loosed, a link so potent it managed to cut through the drug's constant veil. She blinked slowly, the only motion she could permit herself just then, and decided that hearing her son discuss his day with her beloved husband made for a fitting end.

The pain eased, at least for an instant. She knew the unseen portal loomed just beyond her vision, and regretted that she had no choice but to pass through. The remaining moments were too precious, too few. She counted out her small, slight breaths like a miser. She wished for a hundred thousand more.

Josiah dozed in the corner chair. She tilted her head a fraction, not far enough to sharpen her discomfort, just enough to glance his way. The light through her window penetrated his dark skin and revealed a broad swath of freckles that covered both cheeks. His strong features were turned to melted tallow by time's careless hand. But the potency was still there, and the goodness. He slumbered until she called upon him again. The gift of a silent friend. She settled back, grateful for that final opportunity to cherish the remarkable souvenir of a welcoming heart.

Kimberly and Carey and Sylvie sat together at the room's other side. They chatted with the ease of lifelong friends. Even Sylvie was softened by the caring natures shown to her by Beth's youngest and Buddy's newfound love. Beth found an utter contentment in watching them sit there and giggle like children.

Beth's attention returned to the man laid out on the other side of the wall. She was so grateful for Jack's willingness to bend, to break, to redefine his heart's direction. She loved Jack more, now, than she ever had before. Her feelings remained undimmed, even by this constant wash of drugs. Now, when each breath was a soft triumph, when Jack was lost beyond reach, he still held her. He always would.

"Momma?"

She smiled, but did not speak. The three of them looked at her, the daughter who had sung the melody needed to bring her father back to his senses. The woman who held her son's heart with such fierce passion she shunned safety to aid him. And the older daughter whose own heart might just be touched by the light shining in those two faces.

And still, Buddy's voice resonated through the wall behind her head.

"Momma, do you need something?"

Beth tried to shake her head, but the effort was too much. It didn't matter. The truth was, these precious young people were all the affirmation one heart would ever need. Despite all the imperfections and errors her life could possibly hold, she had still achieved what was most important. She breathed, she released, and she almost heard a voice declare, Well done.

MOONDUST LAKE

Davis Bunn

ABOUT THIS GUIDE

The suggested questions are included to enhance
your group's reading of Davis Bunn's

MOONDUST LAKE

DISCUSSION QUESTIONS

1. Buddy decides to leave his father's company at a critical moment. The timing of his move threatens the company's future. Was he right to act as he did? How would you have handled this if you were in his shoes?

2. Often in moving from the story's creation to packaging, the publisher's sales and marketing team will revise a title so that it better suits the overall scope and feel of a series. The working title of this novel was 'Prodigal Father'. Which do you prefer? Or would you have chosen a different title altogether?

3. Why do you think Beth Helms leaves her husband? Do you think she made the right move? Did she accomplish what she hoped to?

4. The crux of this story comes down to six people all facing a need to leave their past behind. Discuss this issue from the following five perspectives:

   a. Buddy Helms, needing to develop his identity free from his father's influence;
   b. Jack Helms, needing to retreat from his earlier dark actions;
   c. Carey Helms, whose fractured relationship with her father influences her choice of men;
   d. Kimberly Sturgiss, who remains burdened by the actions of a man who did not deserve her love;
   e. Your own situation, the present versus the past.

5. Jack Helms is vehemently opposed to the establishment of a counseling center. How do feel about this? Is there

room in your community for such a place? Would it draw the community together, or force it further apart?

6. How does Beth Helms' ill health affect her fractured family?

7. Throughout the Miramar Bay novels—*Miramar Bay*, *Firefly Cove*, and *Moondust Lake*—many different aspects of California have come to light, from Hollywood glamor to the drought-stricken Central Valley, from a lovely coastal resort town to the hills ringing San Luis Obispo. Wine regions, mountains, floods, mudslides . . . Did any of this surprise you?

8. What do you think of the idea that Miramar Bay is a town of second chances? What is it about this town that inspires this concept? Do you agree with it? If Miramar Bay were a real town instead of a fictional one, would you be tempted to visit?